No Limit

Holly Childs

HOLOGRAM

Published by Hologram,
an imprint of Express Media Inc.

Express Media
176 Little Lonsdale St
Melbourne VIC 3000

expressmedia.org.au
hologrambooks.com.au

Copyright © Holly Childs, 2014

All rights reserved. No part of this publication may be reproduced, stored in a retrieval system, or transmitted in any form by any means electronic, mechanical, photocopying, recording or otherwise without the prior consent of the publisher.

Cover design by Elwyn Murray
Printed and bound by Griffin Press

The publisher thanks Adolfo Aranjuez and Michelle Allan

National Library of Australia Cataloguing-in-Publication entry:

No limit / Holly Childs.
9781742707907 (paperback)
A823.4

 Distributed by Hardie Grant

 Express Media is a proud member of The Small Press Network

 The paper this book is printed on is certified against the Forest Stewardship Council® Standards. Griffin Press holds FSC chain of custody certification SGS-COC-005088. FSC promotes environmentally responsible, socially beneficial and economically viable management of the world's forests.

This project has been assisted by the Australian Government through the Australia Council for the Arts, its arts funding and advisory body.

When Misty gets to Anahera's at 2 am after riding from the Hunua Ranges, fifty kilometres south-east, she strips down to her thermals. She's got a temperature from overexertion, exhaustion. A gawky teen with kind of bad skin, young and conscious of it, she goes straightaway to the bathroom to brush her tangly hair. When she comes back out she tells me that if she were truly herself, she would be out drawing on walls and putting up posters for the rave that weekend. Then she drifts to fucked-up sleep so heavy she spasms and pops, her limbs set at seemingly impossible angles, face crunched up; I've just folded out Anahera's sofa to sleep on and Misty's spread out all across it. I don't want to touch her because I've just met her and she's a girl, so I grab for a cushion by her head, trying hard not to disrupt her or even look at her, and I guess I make a sort of bed for myself on the floor next to the sofa. I reach up and turn out the light.

Next morning we sit in the kitchen with Anahera and some guy named Dick, who slept in her room the night before. I'm reading a eulogy for the Beastie Boy who died a while ago that's in an oldish issue of *Rolling Stone*. Maybe we look empty, or like we just can't care for ourselves, because Anahera keeps offering Misty and me sips of her coffee. Dick cuts slivers off his peach, giving a slice to Misty, then a slice to me, back and forth until there isn't any peach left for him. He sucks the stone.

After those two leave for work, Misty bursts into giggles because she says her last girlfriend was quiet, just like me, and she misses her. Then she tears up, says she's used to having someone to share her sleeping bag with. Dick has left his mobile phone on the kitchen table. Misty fingers its screen, puts it in her pocket. Through tears she says, 'It's sad that we'll be dead one day and the whole world will be gone.' Then she takes a deep breath and asks me if I have any money.

We catch a bus together up to her old high school, which I guess she still lays some claim to as she points to the tags she's done on all of the walls, though she says the bulk of them have been buffed. We walk up a mountain track behind her school and when we get to the summit I ask her why there is a fucking huge dent in it and she says, 'It's the crater, dummy. This is a volcano. All mountains around Auckland are volcanoes.' She points out about eight more across the horizon and tells me their names. 'That's Maungakiekie, or One Tree Hill, that one's Māngere mountain, that's Mt Hobson, that's Mt Victoria, and that over there, the one with the clouds around it, that's Rangitoto.' There's a gang of old people sitting at a bench drinking sparkling wine out of plastic cups, wearing Xmas hats, tinsel twisted around their sunglasses, and I'm feeling kind of photosensitive like the tinsel is burning marks in my eyes so I close them. Misty takes a picture of me on Dick's phone and I'm squinting in the sun, kind of pulling at my ear.

When she shows it to me, in the background of the photo it looks like Sky Tower is coming out the top of my head.

On the way back down the mountain Dick's phone starts ringing but Misty doesn't answer it, just hands it to me and keeps walking. It's Anahera. While I'm trying to explain to her why we have Dick's phone I lose my feet or misjudge an angle and slip about five metres down a loose rocky slope and Misty laughs. Like, points and laughs, a real belly one. Shocked, feeling knocked out but miraculously still conscious, I tell Anahera I have to go and hang up. I hobble over to Misty, scratches and filthy cuts down the whole right-hand side of my body. If I'm like her girlfriend, I feel like she should care that I fell, but she just laughs at me while she brushes the rocks out of my grazes, wipes the dirt away, gives me a drink from her water flask. Then, her back against my feet in a patch of sunlight, she promptly falls asleep.

I look up at the sun through my eyelashes, like rainbows radiating through fern fronds and palms, until my eyes hurt again. Then I watch Misty sleep for a while. I get out my journal, find my cousin's phone number, and text her from Dick's phone to say that she can reach me on this number. She's meant to be flying through Auckland on her way to Sydney, but she said she wasn't sure if she would have a chance to leave the airport and meet me. Then I go back to watching Misty, this cute cat I can never touch, twisted around my ankles, and then when she wakes up she asks me if I can rap.

I think about just leaving with Misty. We could hitchhike up north or I could get a bike here. I already know I love her and I don't want it to end. We'd go to the beach together, eat properly, maybe I could get a place on the water, a job, a reason to be. I could look after this girl, and together we could make everything else disappear.

We walk together into town and as we go people stop us to say that we're cartoons; Misty translates, they all sound like goblin fairies to me. I ask what they mean and she says, 'They think we look good together, Haydn.' Misty is hunting for an easy way into an abandoned warehouse in the Viaduct for this rave she's planning, and she makes and receives several calls from rave co-organisers on Dick's phone. On the property, but not yet inside the warehouse, a security guard catches us, tells us to move along, but Misty says, 'I remember you from high school, you do graffiti.' After that the guard leaves us alone.

When Misty is confident that she's found a way in, we get out of the warehouse and onto a bus back to Anahera's apartment. We sit up the back and Misty takes my hands and pulls me close until her hair is soft and hot against my ear. We talk with our temples touching. She thanks me for helping her in the warehouse, even though I'd just stood there, then she points out graffiti on buildings outside the bus, her voice vibrating softly around my skull, and when she asks me if I can read what the pieces say I tell her I can't read throwie font, because at that moment I want a very small world, just her and me and nothing else, no buildings, no tags, nothing. She starts mansplaining to me how to read the tags, but I like it. Up the back of that bus we talk and touch like slutty kissing cousins with secret glances and circles of breath. Slow motion. A new world. I brush my lips against her cheek and she roughly pulls my hand up to her face and kisses my ragged palm, and then each of the scrapes and grazes all up my arm. But she is inattentive, like she's kissing just for herself, as though I'm not even there, or real, and then Dick's phone rings and she takes the call.

We get off at Anahera's stop. Misty and I walk the backstreets to the apartment and she jumps up to grab feijoas off neighbourhood trees. I try to take her hand but she pushes me away and picks up a big stick to scrape against the fences we pass, making a sound like a giant güiro that sets off all the dogs in the area.

When we get back to Anahera's she yells hello from her room, but Misty and I go straight to the lounge room to rest. Misty lies on the sofa and closes her eyes. I sit beside her, staring at the wall trying to recover my sense of self. Misty rolls over, her face an inch away from my body, and she says she likes my poetry but that I should write it up on walls instead of trapping it inside of books. I guess she found my journal somehow, even though I keep it right at the bottom of my bag and we have literally been together the whole time since meeting the night before. Anahera comes into the lounge room and grabs Dick's phone out of Misty's hands because she's texting again. Anahera tells us that she isn't our mum, she isn't going to keep looking after us, she isn't even going to yell at us for taking the phone, but if we are going to keep staying with her we have to do some work. 'I'm having a party tomorrow night and I want you two to handle drinks and nibbles, can you do that?' She tells us to go to New World and buy some supplies, she can't keep pampering us at the breakfast table forever.

Misty shoots me a look of pure fucking terror.

'The theme of the party is apocalypse,' says Anahera. 'So maybe think of some snacks and drinks that scream suicide cult, environmental disaster, plague. And, guys, you have to apologise to Dick for taking his phone, he's coming over now.' Anahera keeps talking as she walks away, unlocking the door for Dick on the way back to her bedroom.

'But tomorrow night's the rave, I have to be there to set up,' Misty says, to me.

Dick stomps down the hallway and into the lounge room. He looks at us. 'So, did I miss any calls today?'

'Nope.'

'Not in the whole day? No one called me?'

Anahera comes in, says, 'Dick, I'm having a party tomorrow night. It's apocalypse theme, wear something scary.'

'Oh, but I was just going to invite you to the double Armageddon feature at the DIY drive-in, but okay, yeah, I'll come to your party, sure.' Dick does a weird tilted-head grimace, which is maybe the closest he can physically get to forming a traditional smile. Really stiff. 'I'll go to the drive-in by myself.'

Ash Rumble is on a suspension bridge following or waiting for someone, a girl. Green and red lights oscillate beneath her through mist, blinking in sequence. She reaches her hand out and touches skin, a barcode? A barcode tattoo on the arm of a man emerging from the fog, the mist, he shakes her hand, the suspension bridge bounces up and down in time. The air is thick. As she steps closer to the edge, the bridge gives way beneath her. She's in free fall until she myoclonic jerks awake in economy class next to a guy with a barcode tattooed on his bicep and Fudge hair product in his long, beautiful hair. He is wearing G-Star Raw jeans and nothing else. He's sleeping. His body, oiled, flecked with glitter, is belted to the seat. In his hands he holds a broadsheet newspaper dated 17 November 2012, though that was weeks ago. The banner headline reads ASH OBSCURES GLOBAL FLIGHT. Ash looks out the window of the 737 she's on and thinks: It's always a clear day above the clouds. But then she looks closer and sees a flock of CGI bluebirds frolicking all around the wing and thinks either there's a really high-quality transparent LCD TV finish installed in this 737 window or… she presses into the palm of her hand and it kind of smooshes like ripe banana and then—Ash wakes up again and thinks: A dream within a dream, that is so tacky. Though now that she's definitely awake, the guy next to her is wearing a shirt, cool. He leans towards her and whispers, 'Everyone shows their true colours above the clouds.' The plane lurches. The guy tries to look past Ash, out the window, to see what is happening outside the plane. Ash gets a text message from an unknown number asking her if she wants to join the mile-high club, which is weird, because her phone is on airplane mode.

When she gets into Auckland Airport at 10.45 pm, the AirCon check-in counter is closed and Ash spends a couple of hours dozing in the departure hall on a bench, with the straps of her bags twisted around her own arms and the bench's leg. At either 2 am or 5 am, times proffered by Ash's iPhone and MacBook Pro respectively, Ash wakes up, looks over, and now there's a line of people waiting at the AirCon counter. It's still dark outside. She tweets: 'To delete Facebook & start anew, to populate a new FB profile with only "friends" who I am actually friends with, to delete FB 4ever?' She checks Facebook, scrolls Instagram for about forty seconds, and then she goes to check in for her next flight.

A girl in front of Ash in the check-in line is sitting on the edge of a luggage trolley, her back against a stack of hard-case luggage. She's talking to a guy in a sweat-stained cowboy hat, possibly Australian, about her t-shirt, which has a man's face on it, possibly Julian Assange's. The guy is saying, 'Well, I'm just impressed that you know who he is,' and she's saying, 'Yeah, I mean, everyone does…' The girl sitting on the luggage trolley starts rifling through a translucent pink tote with golden clasps and she gets out a big box of Rococo chocolates and offers him one. 'It was a going-away present,' she says with her mouth full. She has a nondescript accent and an iPad balanced on her knees. She looks like she bleaches her eyebrows.

Two guys behind Ash, a couple, talk excitedly about what they are going to do when they get to Paris. It's so trippy that some people have literally never been to Paris before, thinks Ash, and then she mentally checks her own privilege. Ash wonders why all these people are transiting through Auckland though, because it seems like pretty much the edge of the Earth, Middle-earth. The only person Ash knows in Auckland is her cousin Haydn, and he only just moved here like four days ago. The couple behind her is now discussing which of them should look after their bags while the other goes out the front to smoke a cigarette and assess the air quality. They decide to take turns.

Ash checks in, heads to immigration. She looks at her phone: 3.18 am, three retweets. In front of her is the girl from the check-in line, her iPad still on in the palm of her hand. She's patting the screen, swanning the thing around like she's searching for unlocked wifi. She's really tall, probably 6'3". A border official leans over the rope and tells the girl, in a relaxed way, to kindly put her device away. This border official sounds just like a little elf. New Zealand accents are obnoxious.

Ash is filling out her immigration form while waiting in the line but the biro she's using is running out of ink. She can't tell how long she should say she's going to spend in Australia since she's planning on overstaying indefinitely. A family standing behind her discuss the food they think they're going to eat when they get to Los Angeles while complaining about how long everything is taking. The way they're talking about food it's like they think LA is on the other side of the immigration line and not a twelve-hour flight away. The tall girl in front of her gets to the front of the line, goes to an immigration window. 'I'm gonna eat some waffles,' says a kid behind Ash. 'Waffles and chicken with syrup and a hash brown. Three hash browns and real hot sauce and bacon. American cheese and Peanut Butter M&M's in a milkshake on pancakes. Lemonade.'

Ash is distracted by a guard saying, 'Well, for starters, the passport you are carrying shows someone who is clearly a male, with grey-black eyes and a nose-ring, and I'm really struggling to reconcile that with what I'm seeing here in front of me.' It's the tall girl getting totally ragged out by the border guard. Soon there are like five cops crowding around her. 'People change,' she says and tries pushing through the cops and off into the departure lounge. Ash is fixated, disturbed by her inability to mentally extricate herself from this situation, she's standing there watching a complete stranger get interrogated. Can they actually deny her exit from New Zealand? Like, why bother? Ash cannot look away, trying to work out who this girl is, what the fuck her deal is, what the fuck is going on? The butchest cop grabs the girl's arm and wrenches her back, pulling up her sleeve. He's touching something on her inner arm.

'Can we scan this?' the cop spits, not to the girl, but to another male cop who already has some sort of laser pointer out and aimed at the girl's arm. The thing emits an indeterminate retro modem-style tone, then after a moment a chirpy beep. The girl goes limp for a second. The scene is so car crash, and it doesn't help that the girl is like flawless. Still gripping her arm, the cop triple-takes at his screen, shakes the girl awake, abruptly drops her arm and says, 'Bon voyage, Ms... aaah, Madam. Please have a safe and happy trip and come back soon!' He sounds like he's from the tourism board. The girl wanders off, through duty-free, not looking particularly unnerved. The green sign above the terminal she went through clicks to red but all five cops stay in the booth, crowded around the computer, faces glowing. Another immigration officer says, 'Next please,' rings a little bell, and Ash rolls her carry-on over to his window.

In the departure lounge, Ash takes a pill to go to sleep and lies down across some seats. But after a couple of vague hours she's buzzing. She wants to tweet 'Fuck u Stilnox, Worst Pharm Ever,' but her phone isn't doing international roaming for some reason. She sits up, the airport carpet is a shifting green and black fern repeat. Gangs of surf bros wander about in thongs and board shorts. Ash feels like whenever you see anyone interesting in an airport, they usually end up being on your flight, and she spots the really tall girl sitting on a bench like two metres away. Ash tries to make eye contact, thinks about going to introduce herself, but then she totally loses it and instead tries to not make any eye contact at all. It's like, when you first see a girl like that, just knowing that she exists is enough, you're almost afraid that she'll return your attention, because then what? It's fucked up, you are full, the girl is a projection. She comes from inside of you. It won't last. But then you go deeper and you take in her secondary artefacts, reality, things you know you haven't invented because they never seemed remotely cute or appealing until you saw them in proximity to this girl, this girl! A blue glitter-jelly bracelet around her arm and the broken zip on her backpack, her coffee order—but not her name—scrawled on the side of a cup, a little scar thing behind her ear. And in your heart and your mind you start storing fragments of the girl, consequential or not, they're all perfect. And over time these elements add up and you want to know her name, you want to see her smile. You wish to be the one making her smile. But concurrently you know it's not safe or fair to store your desire in another person, a girl you've never met. Being capable of making eye contact would probably be a good start.

But behind her she can hear someone talking, fiercely detracting from her admittedly fairly banal fantasy. 'She just does heaps of reblogs, like, she adds no content at all. She never does comments, she doesn't like anything, her entire personal brand is built off of other people's hard work, totally uncredited, like, I don't care because I mean, I guess that's just what you have to do if you don't have any ideas of your own but really, like, how difficult is it to just *not* press delete on someone else's source info? And you know what else? I think she queues her posts.'

An announcement: 'Due to unforeseen circumstances, some flights have now been delayed. Please hold on for further updates.' Fucking great. Ash drops her head back and bangs heads with a middle-aged guy with a ponytail, who still doesn't stop bitching about some Tumblr noob over the phone. He's rubbing the back of his head though, looks more pissed off. She apologises and goes over to the window. All that's out there are a bunch of huge HSBC adverts and airport crewmembers driving their boneless reptilian baggage carts around the airfield. There's a haze in the air, orange lights shining through. Ash watches a plane come in to land at an acute angle and it seems to hit its left wingtip against the runway. Ash flinches, holds out for the crash, but there is none.

She opens her eyes again to see the plane happily bouncing further down the runway, the left wingtip slightly crumpled, maybe. The crew holding sticks on the airfield are running though, talking on radios, waving arms, covering their faces, although perhaps this behaviour is normal. Lego figurines. Inside the terminal each flight on the departures information board rapidly bleeps in turn from ON TIME, BOARDING, and CHECK-IN to CANCELLED, CANCELLED, CANCELLED. Flick, flick, flick. Ash has a sense, coming from somewhere external to her, that she needs to stop lagging. Snap out of it. Ash looks over to where the tall girl was sitting but she's gone.

Volcanic lava and ash spew into the atmosphere around Auckland and Ash walks back through the terminal, dragging her bags. She wants to have a real conversation with the people at the AirCon counter about what's going on but the queue is too long. A representative from the airline walks up and down the line handing out $12 meal vouchers and 250MB 3G dongles to each 'inconvenienced traveller' since the airport wifi has dropped out. This won't last long. She gets the dongle and gets on her MacBook Pro and tweets, 'Stuck in a limitless delay in AKL airport with unspecified "situation" affecting all flights' then 'Provisional emergency accommodation being installed between water coolers and vending machines. Nomads' backpacks prolapsing onto info desk' and then 'Need more Stilnox, let me sleep!' Almost immediately she gets two favourites and one retweet.

Ash tries calling her cousin Haydn but she can't get through. She googles 'Auckland flight delays news' and finds a visualisation of a volcano eruption. An interactive map on the *Guardian* website shows clouds of smoke and silt, ash skidding across the Southern Hemisphere in realtime. The streaks are shaded white through turquoise to emerald, graphing the intensity of the treatment, but out the window the atmosphere seems unremarkable, just a light haze.

The terminal is packed. Ash floats through to an opinion piece on the *Guardian* entitled 'Imagine a World Without Planes' and then another article called 'Apocalypse Soon,' which correlates this Auckland natural disaster with the end of the Mayan calendar. A suit has unplugged one of the airport's massage chairs to charge his phone, he's slumping between the two chairs, tie loosened, sweating, all caricature. Ash needs water. She tweets her flight number to @AirCon and asks when she can expect her flight to be rescheduled for. The $12 voucher just gets her a fucking grilled sandwich, no change. Then there's a pretty loud rumble, like an earthquake only the ground doesn't shake. She has to get to Sydney. She dials Haydn again and gets through this time, but the line is clipped, their voices staccato. Ash is in the air. Everyone is too hot. People are wearing streetwear, beachwear, because Australia? New Zealand. Same thing? All flights are grounded.

'Haydn! I'm so happy I got through to you. Help me out, cuz. I need a place to stay, hang out with me, occupy me until I get to fly out again.'

'Wait, who are you?' asks Haydn. A guy walks by Ash wearing trackpants tucked into Doc Martens.

'It's Ash, your cousin!'

'I don't know any Ash. Did Misty give you this number?'

'No, my cousin Haydn did.'

'Okay. I guess I know that guy, do you want me to take a message for him?'

'No I really need to meet with him ASAP, my flight just

got cancelled. Do you know where he is now? Can I contact him directly?'

'I don't know where he is, but maybe you should come and meet me. You sound pretty messed up. Come to 354 Karangahape Road. I'll be at a gallery called Ne Plus Ultra. Come in and ask for Dick.'

'Dick?'

'Yes, Dick.'

The really tall girl walks past Ash. Ash wants to follow her but all of her stuff is spread out around her, laptop open on her knees and the phone reception is so bad that she's using all her energy trying to osmosis the info this Dick just gave her. So she just sits there. Jetlag. Watching this dream girl walk away, out of the airport, out of her life.

Okay, 354 Karanga-something. Ash takes a No-Doz to speed up. She packs up her shit and goes to find a taxi.

ASH GETS TO Ne Plus Ultra. Under an oversized version of an old-style filament light globe a handful of people sit on yoga balls, sipping from ergonomic sports-water bottles, tapping at retro orange and turquoise Apple laptops. They look up when she walks in. A tiny dog rushes over barking at a high pitch. The girl sitting closest to where Ash is leans over and hands her a roomsheet and introduces the teacup poodle, who is struggling to breathe, as Fuchsia Dream. 'You can pat him.' Ash introduces herself and asks for Dick. A guy with a beard bounces out from behind the iBook he is working on, shakes Ash's hand and offers her a biscuit called a Tim Tam.

Dick invites Ash to have a look at the current exhibition, called *Not Dreams*. The roomsheet has a quote from an American art critic saying that this show 'answers the question we've all been asking: "Can an artist working in the digital realm break through to the mainstream?" With the resounding answer: at this point, not necessarily.'

Dick asks Ash what she's doing in Auckland.

'I was just meant to be transiting, but I think a volcano just started erupting. My airline couldn't tell me when my flight would be rescheduled for.'

'Ah, but so far Rangitoto is just smoking, technically not yet erupting. It will though. Funny day for it to happen. I mean, you probably know that the "Mayan" "apocalypse" as a "thing" was contrived in the seventies by a couple of white American brothers who were high as beeps, tripping in the "Amazon", who came to believe that the weight of their psilocybin experience was such that the whole world would end when they said it would. But hey, it is fun to imagine apocalypse. Explosions! Disaster! Death. It's kind of exciting, don't you think?'

'Ummm…' Ash pivots away from Dick, looks at the show. There's a work by PB PR that's melted pirated DVDs of *The Cremaster Cycle* moulded into rings that have PB PR etched onto them, a work by someone distantly involved with *Dis Magazine*, something from a local experimental fashion collective called Pauline. A work by Amalia Ulman that is decals affixed to glass panels on a door propped sideways against a wall, including Volcom, Independent, Roxy, DC Shoes and Etnies logos, the woman symbol and some stars, a crescent moon and the zodiac symbol for Capricorn. A piece by Clara Chon that is a round deerskin fur bag studded with rivets forming a sad face next to a quote from Blair Waldorf that says, 'Fashion is the most powerful art there is. It's movement, design and architecture all in one. It shows the world who we are and who we'd like to be.'

'Do you know this artist?' asks Dick, pointing at an inflatable plastic ring with various sports-water brands' logos tessellated across it.

Ash says she doesn't and instead mentions that the *Guardian* website said the volcano had been throwing up ash and rocks, and that its smoke was at three thousand metres.

'Ah, yes, and I expect it will get worse,' says Dick with a smile. 'They haven't even put out an evacuation order yet.'

The final work in *Not Dreams* is an audio piece that plays on a loop, a woman's voice autotuned over slow techno. 'Hey Porsche, I'm at a weird rave in a palace with very high-quality speakers. Everyone in here looks like a total troll because we're all wearing all white, like we should be drinking milk, like we should be pigging out on vanilla ice-cream sundaes, I know right? Instead it's bubbly, this is Paris baby, so champagne must have seemed the stronger leitmotiv to somebody upstairs. [A giggle.] And on cue a girl wanders past eating a baguette. Under strobe. No one is distinguishable from anyone else. Like seriously, imagine a rave filled with people dancing with dripping ice-creams. A rave with no exit.' The catalogue essay likens this piece to the work of both Laurie Anderson and Simon Reynolds but Ash isn't buying it. She thinks it's totally fucked. 'But you know what? This rave in a palace needs more Buffalo boots. Ravers here are rocking a lot of purely forgettable looks, guys. Nothing is distinguishable from anything else. Polite men. I watch white bottles skit around the dance floor, but actually the bottles are prisms of light and not redeemable for fun in 3D. [A giggle.] A boy walks past wearing earphones with a string of diamantes hanging from each ear. Like an earring but balanced inside like [she whispers] inner ear crystals.'

This audio keeps looping over and over, like horrible, like shut up. Like jetlag. Ash feels like she's been standing in the same spot for hours and she wants to leave the gallery, so she asks Dick where she can get something to eat. He says, 'You look really familiar, and that's not a pick-up line.'

'Maybe you've seen me in tagged photos, we both know Haydn.'

'Yeah but I don't really know Haydn, I just met him yesterday. I've seen you close-up though. In real life. I'm just finishing up here, let's go together, someplace else. There's a pizza joint just down the road.'

Ash is into it, but then Dick puts on a leather trench coat and Ash suddenly feels a strong steampunk vibe radiating off him. She is flooded with a really specific kind of fear, a fear she associates with clowns. She's not personally afraid of clowns but she gets why they are scary, and Dick in steampunk regalia is scary in exactly that way. Ash doesn't want anything to do with this guy anymore but, in a strange country with a volcano haze in the air, she has few options. 'Um Dick, is there a way we could try to contact Haydn again?' she asks.

Dick drapes a fox fur over his shoulders, Ash's heart drops. Now she is not just scared but also grossed out. Dick slings on his black rubber backpack and an old-timey train drivers' hat, and this is the point when Ash realises that she is officially in too deep with a tintype dude she's just met who claims he knows Haydn, but only just. Dick says goodbye to everyone still working on the yoga balls. The girl who gave Ash the roomsheet asks, 'Oh, you don't want to stay for the discussion group? Tonight we're reading Tiqqun.' But Dick just waves at her and walks out of the gallery.

'I don't think Haydn has a phone, right? But I've run into him three separate times in the past twenty-four hours, so if you hang with me we'll probably just find him again by chance,' Dick says. He guides Ash to his Nissan jeep pig hunter, once touching her butt, possibly by accident. He tells her he bought this car off an actual pig hunter. 'It's a

Nissan Patrol SWB 4×4 4.0 LT manual, ideal for shooting, hunting and four-wheel driving. Rock climbing, farm work, mud, sand dunes, paddock bashing. Tipping cows. Sploshing.' He chuckles.

They sit in his jeep. Dick shuffles a deck of cards. 'This is a tarot deck, do you know tarot? I want you to pick a card and from there we'll decide where we should go.' He fans the deck in front of Ash, wafting a stench of citrus and fresh perspiration as he goes. She pulls The Hanged Man. He says that that's actually a good sign. 'If you look at the picture, he's hanging by his feet not his neck. This card symbolises patience, acceptance. Seems absolutely perfect for your situation.' He does a deranged lopsided grin.

Then Dick pulls a card, Death. 'Ah, good, psychological transformation. A fantastic card.' His car is filled with flowers, leaves. 'I've just had an idea, let's go to the drive-in, there's an Armageddon double feature on. Two apocalypse movies back to back.' Ash has nowhere else to go. Dick starts the engine.

When you are initially attracted to someone based only on the fact that they seem inoffensive and are willing to spend time with you, and then that person asserts their identity by putting on a weird scarf or telling you that they enjoy the complete oeuvre of the Goo Goo Dolls, you might start hating them to make up for the fact that five minutes earlier you were prepared to share your thoughts with them, your vulnerability. Dick hums along to the radio. He explains to Ash in a ribbony way that his biological occupation is floristry, that's what's with all the flowers in the car, but that being a gallery assistant is his ambient profession, his one true love. There's a photo of a blonde girl blu-tacked onto the dash, kind of hard to see in the dark.

In this light Dick looks like James Franco but Ash wishes he looked like James Duval. She squints, it doesn't help. They drive past a football field where figures are stumbling around with long shadows. Everything tingles red.

'Who's this?' Ash asks about the girl in the photo on the dash.

'What? Oh. She's someone I made an app with once. But she ripped me off and now I hate her,' Dick says, watching the road.

'What happened?'

'Tom from MySpace, that's what happened.'

'Oh, everybody's first friend!'

'Yeah well actually he sucks and,' pointing to the photo, 'she sucks and fuck their fucking business bullshit and I hope they both die in hell. Okay? You want the story?'

'Sure, I mean…'

'Well, I was developing an app with that girl. Content overruns, "Gazers" we called them. Code that sneaks over existing data, on Google and Facebook and any other websites a user might be doing searches on. The concept was to track and aggregate the user's search history and throw up a morphing realtime montage of the kinds of things the user routinely searches for and looks at. To put that information into any unused or vacant pixel-areas on each website the user surfs, into any blank space on websites. Sidebars, headers, backgrounds. So this app performed as what we referred to as a "personal cybermirror".' Finger quotes. 'What we were doing was letting the user clearly see what they are already searching for, which is reasonably innocuous if all you're looking for is coffee-ground vomiting, baby animals, boys with faces that look like pizza, but if you're the kind of person who's looking up something a bit harder it might be a scary ride. We thought the program would inspire people to log off. It seemed logical that when users finally saw themselves reflected in collaged approximations of the inane shit they were searching for anyway but amplified, remixed, they'd grow some sense of self-awareness, self-consciousness even. But actually what we discovered in the testing phase was that people like to share. Almost every test user we worked with was entirely happy to show the world exactly what they were up to online, even if it's just researching natural herpes creams. Do you know this word "narcissism"? Google offered to buy it off us before we'd even finished the prototype, they were tossing up big numbers.' Dick shrugs. 'But we said no fucking way, pigs, you can't take us, we're gonna release it open-source. But the night before we did, by chance, this girl ran into Tom from MySpace in a real-life bar. They had a couple of drinks together, she sold the program to him, and I'm pretty sure they finger banged.' Dick mimes stabbing himself in the heart. 'I don't know how much money she got out of it but she's been living in Dubai for a while now, driving a bubble-pink Koenigsegg CCXR.' Dick indicates, drives slowly down a dark unsealed track, stops at a big tin shed, drives into the tin shed, keeps telling the story, idling in complete darkness, ignoring a faint rumbling which may be the volcano. 'And I hate her.' A movie screen brightens through the front window. They're at the drive-in.

'Wow, algorithms are so passé,' Ash mumbles.

'What?'

'You keep her photo up though? You must still like her a bit.'

'Yeah I keep her photo up, why wouldn't I? She meant a lot to me at one point, and life is long and complicated and things don't always work out neatly and she's sick now and I'm sorry for her pain but there's nothing I can do for her but I'm not going to just rip up a photo of a sick girl, fuck!' Dick is doing extreme eye contact in the semi-dark. He turns off the engine.

The first movie is starting, it's *Melancholia*. Emerald green ash floats through the projection like glitter. It's not that dense but the audience cough and clear their throats. A gang of boys next to Dick and Ash sit on the bonnet of their car passing around and huffing on asthma puffers, beating their chests, singing along to Miley Cyrus, Angel Haze. A skinny guy wearing a large indie band t-shirt and silver-riveted nightvision goggles walks past carrying choctops.

Ash's mind returns to her concern with Dick's complete look: leather trench coat, greasy black hair, a beard, scuffed leather boots, black jeans with an oil sheen, black rubber backpack. He also has a few extra trinkets including a Bless No. 38 iPhone 4 cover that looks like a rock. A hard heavy rock that feels big in your hand. Dick explains, 'Yeah it's functional, every form is functional. That's a semiotic issue about which many people are misguided. The exact name of this product I don't know, I bought it from the last show at Ne Plus Ultra. I can reach all the buttons and the rear-facing camera is not obscured. It's an advanced version of the kind of fake rock you get at two-dollar shops to hide your house keys under but it's got my iPhone in it instead. It's virtually shatterproof.' The fox fur rests over his shoulders, its glass eyes glint gold.

Dick leans over to her and asks if she can see the movie properly. He whispers into her ear that he finds Kirsten Dunst very sexy in this role, but he keeps calling her other names; first Claire Danes, then Daniel Radcliffe, Fred Durst, Kristen Stewart, then finally Kerry Packer. He says he wishes he were her groom, or at least the boss's nephew. 'She's so fucking depressed,' he says, sniffing Ash's hair, or neck.

Ash leans in closer to Dick, then they hear a rap at the window and everybody in the vicinity turns around, the boys huffing Ventolin, a group of girls with looks halfway between The Baby-Sitters Club and Bratz dolls, all of them turning to see the full-service roving candy-bar attendant wiggling his finger at Dick, motioning for him to wind down his window and buy some snacks. Ash sticks her hand in her pocket in search of cash but Dick has already said 'fuck off' to the roving candy-bar attendant, miming to him aggressively with just one finger.

The car directly in front of Dick's is covered in bumper stickers that say things like 21 DEC 2012 ARMAGEDDON: JUDGEMENT DAZE and Dick points, 'Geez, if you really thought tonight was the last night on Earth, why the hell would you spend it at the movies?' He inhales Ash's neck.

'Isn't that what you're doing?' says Ash.

'Do you really think I believe that I'm going to die tonight?' He's doing sex eyes.

'Everything feels out of date.'

'What, Ash?'

'Nothing, I mean, you seem like a pretty kooky guy, you're certainly foreshadowing something. Your outfit is expressing things that your mouth isn't…'

'Well boohoo, slut, you think I'm a future dead guy with weird clothes? Why don't you just suck my dick and put me out of this misery. I am looking after you here, you'd still be alone waiting at the airport if it wasn't for me.'

'Excuse me, what? Who says that? I don't know you. Yeah I'm stuck here, but this is bullshit. You're not doing me a favour, you're being totally lecherous and I can't leave. And now I can't trust you and I don't know anyone else.' She slaps a mosquito.

'Look, I'm sorry. You can definitely trust me, I'm a gentleman. I was joking. And you always have options, Ash, in every situation. Don't be such a victim, you're not trapped. You can leave whenever you want.'

'Dick, I literally cannot leave. I'm stuck in Auckland, stuck in your car. It's night-time, we're either in the outer suburbs or straight-up countryside. I can definitely hear sheep, there's a volcano erupting just over there, I'm hungry and I don't have anywhere to stay tonight.' Wind rushes through the jeep's open windows, blows in and around the car; swirling dust and haze. Their hair is blowing into their faces, everything is dramatic, they're both totally antsy, like, what the fuck am I doing here especially if this is the last night ever, which it kind of feels like it might be. But Dick interprets this tension between them as exclusively sexual. He grabs Ash's arm and pulls her across to his seat but her leg hits against the gear stick and she pushes him away. 'Not a gentleman!' She takes a deep breath, then coughs.

'This girl,' Ash says, jabbing at the photo again. 'What does she do in Dubai?'

'Yeah, I actually am a gentleman, that was ah, yeah.' He shrugs, looks out the window. 'Okay, she hooked up with some woman, a princess. I'm not sure which one. I guess they probably drive around, get speeding fines, go to dubstep parties, hang out, do whatever people do when they're "in love".' Finger quotes again. 'But that girl in the photo, she needs Dick too much to stay with a princess for long.' He's pointing to his chest with his thumb, 'So she'll be back. They always come back.'

Kirsten Dunst, Charlotte Gainsbourg and a child actor are holding hands inside a simple structure made of sticks. On the horizon a celestial body grows bigger and bigger until it visibly enters the Earth's atmosphere and then everything on screen ignites. The roving candy-bar attendant comes around again and raps on Dick's window and Dick rolls his eyes. 'Right, you're dead mate.' He hops out of the car. Ash is confused, trying to find a review online that she thought insinuated that at the end of *Melancholia* the planets just bounced off each other like two beach balls, and no one was hurt, but the internet on her phone is going slow and she can hear Dick outside the car kind of growling. There's a thump. She finds the review she was thinking of but in the first paragraph it says, 'A wide shot shows its collision with Earth, which explodes upon impact leaving an imprint no more significant than chalk dust.' Oh, Ash thinks. Chalk dust seems so nothing. It's depressing to realise that the whole world could end so manually, so arbitrarily.

'Ash?' Dick calls out. 'Hey, can you come out here for a minute?' Ash scoots over to the driver's seat and pops the door open, almost clocking Dick because he's on his hands and knees digging in the gravel.

'What's wrong Dick?'

'Ah, just dropped my phone,' he's scrabbling around picking up and then dropping handfuls of pebbles and stones. 'Could you help me out?' He looks up at Ash, his eyes watery, the left one swollen, red. She tilts her phone so light shines on the ground in front of Dick. A Californian nature park comedy apocalypse movie is starting, starring Woody Harrelson as a burnt-out radio hippie. The ash is getting thicker, wiping out the movie screen, and from where they are they can't really see the projection anymore and people around them are throwing popcorn at their own windscreens. Dick hops back into the car and starts the engine.

As they drive out onto the freeway Ash pulls another tarot card, gets The Hanged Man, upside-down, hanging by his neck this time. She doesn't show Dick. He starts again, 'Don't you think it was a mistake that you were called Ash and I just met you, so from my perspective you are crucial to the development of this natural-disaster plot that is fucking up my night, and maybe also the entire world? Like,' he does an affected little cough, 'couldn't you be called Sarah? Do you ever feel like you could just wake up dead tomorrow? This is crazy! Like, is there some kind of greater connection, a bigger story… perhaps you manifested this whole thing in your mind, and if you could just leave Auckland, maybe the volcano ash would clear too and we would all be okay again? Like this "ash",' more finger quotes, 'might just be your little spirit animal? Maybe you just really didn't want to get to where you were flying to next?'

'Ash is not a fucking animal! Look, can you just drive?

And I'll sit here, quietly. Let's go get a burger or something. I'm dying here.' Ash's arms are folded in front of her body. Out the window there are no trees, just fluoro-red lava streaks across a dark landscape.

That Elliot Smith song from *The Royal Tenenbaums* soundtrack starts playing on Dick's smashed iPhone between them. 'I think you're getting a call,' says Ash. The dust in the air is getting really intense. Ash scratches her forearm and sweaty red mud cakes under her fingernails. She's ordinarily repulsed by acoustic guitar but this song's okay, emotional. He's not answering. The phone stops. Now, perhaps because he's inflamed, disturbed, Dick looks a teeny bit like James Duval, maybe. The song begins again from the start, plays for about fifteen seconds, then Dick answers it. He's steering badly and everyone's got their hazard lights on, driving real slow, and he asks Ash if she wants to go to a rave, still on the phone, trying to get the details off whoever's on the other end onto a square of paper that he's holding against the steering wheel with the tip of a tiny IKEA pencil, scribbling crazy, and locusts are slapping, dying against the windscreen. Dick puts the wipers on.

'Why aren't people being evacuated yet? This is totally insane!' says Ash.

'Oh, things will get way worse before that happens,' says Dick.

Just before the party Misty starts vomiting, for a few hours, until it's just bile, until all the blood vessels in her eyelids have burst. And then she puts on this really weird green cosmetic, like too-thick concealer, all around her eyes to mask the bruising. She calls out 'Haydn?' and I go over to the bathroom. She sits me on the edge of the sink, sweeps my hair off my face and tells me to close my eyes.

BEFORE THEY GET TO the rave, Dick stops at his friend's apartment because he says he wants to pick up drugs and drop off flowers. When they pull up out the front he also mentions that his friend is having a party. 'So uh, Haydn might be there,' he says.

Dick walks in and says hey to everybody. Then he asks 'Whose is this acoustic guitar over here?'

A girl wearing gold hotpants and a tank top is all like, 'Mine, Dick!'

Dick asks, 'Do you mind?' He doesn't wait for a response to start strumming the guitar, fingering the strings, humming along. Within seconds he gains confidence, raising his voice at every verse, strumming louder and louder and louder, and soon he's yelling and putting his whole body into the performance. People at the party are nodding along to his folksy acoustic style with an enthusiasm that genuinely surprises Ash. A tall guy in a plain black tracksuit wearing green shit around his eyes offers Ash some 'end of the world' punch, but she declines. She turns away, picks up a copy of *Rolling Stone* magazine off the table and notes that every single band or artist listed on the cover is a man, or men. She doesn't open the magazine. She creeps backwards into a corner by the front door. The girl in the hotpants is really getting into Dick's acoustic guitar playing, jazzing around, shaking her butt and yelling 'whoo!' every few seconds. Ash interrupts her to ask if her building has a rooftop. She does a gesture that says both 'up the stairs' and 'duh'. Ash excuses herself.

Behind her she hears screeching. 'Don't drink the Kool-Aid! You don't want to be as high as we are, this is the true nuclear wasteland! Fuku-fucking-shima apocalypse now!' Some possibly fake machine gun sound effects emanate from the party apartment.

Ash gets to the top of the stairwell, pushes the emergency roof door open and looks around. In the time since she was last outside, the ash in the air seems to have gotten way thicker. In the five minutes she was at the party she'd actually kind of forgotten that it was ashy at all and she was expecting to, you know, be able to get some fresh air. She lies down on a bench up there. The air is sulphuric, smoky, smothering. The sky above is so close, basically red, and swirling. A lava lamp. There are adverts projected into the ash, presumably from clubs downtown. One of them alternately casts RAVER WALK WITH ME and MEET ME AT THE END OF THE WORLD.

Ash can still faintly hear Dick playing that guitar and his friends laughing, clapping along and cheering for him. Her heart rate is really elevated; the acoustic guitar is inescapably resonant. She puts in earbuds and scrolls through her phone until she finds a guided meditation, presses play. 'Hallo. And welcome to this relaxation session. Over the next ten minutes or so you will begin to feel relaxed as you listen to my voice.

But first, here are some guidelines to help you enjoy this session.' It drowns out the guitar noises.

Ash rests her body, which is hollow and still pinging from the caffeine pills she took to balance the Stilnox. She is instructed to breathe out all her negative emotion, to visualise her stressors as colours or shapes gently fading away from her. She watches her thoughts: stranded in Auckland, what may be the last night of life on Earth or at least very definitely the end of life in this city, that guy Dick who seemed cool until he started sexually harassing her and is now playing excruciating acoustic shit. Ash blows it all away. And sees the truth that he's just an eager provincial New Weird America try-hard loser. He has all the signifiers: the furs, the flowers, the oak leaves all through his 'pig hunter', everything. Back to the land. It all floats away.

Ash goes in deeper. She breathes out letting that girl at the airport walk away. That girl seemed like someone Ash could have had a totally harmonious if not downright flirtatious friendship with, and since this morning she's been hoping that this airport girl would just walk past, be there somewhere, but no. Airports are the perfect environment to experience otherworld girls that you will never see again in any other context. The meeting place of a million realities. But if this is how the world ends, at an Auckland apartment party, Ash is gonna be really fucked off. She needs a bang. She progressively breathes out all these feelings and she can physically see negative energy exiting her body through her breath, her eyelids; pulsing rings of red light receding from her frame.

But seriously, every plane got grounded this morning, Ash watched that girl leave the airport. She is probably still somewhere in the city. Maybe Ash could find her. Fall in love. Leave this lame party forever. It's just a little crush.

'This could be a good time to think of a positive affirmation. A message you can repeat to yourself over and over again. Something like: "I am kind to the people around me," or, "I attract the right people into my life at the right times," or, "If the world is to end tonight, then so be it."'

Ash hears the roof door swing open but doesn't look up. Dick must have abandoned his stupid guitar to come and find her, check if she's okay, but it's not relaxing to just break out of a meditation session halfway through, so Dick can wait while a pink warmish glow, like the sun, envelops Ash from her feet, up her legs, through her abdomen, torso, chest, up to her collar, down her arms, to the palms of her hands, all the way down her fingers to the tips, and up her neck, through her whole face, and all over her head, scalp, in and around her brain. Dick can fucking wait. Ash is fluid, warm, concerned with nothing. Nothing. The airport dream girl surfaces into her thoughts again, just for a second. She acknowledges this, but knows that it doesn't have to mean anything. It's just a thought. The airport dream girl floating in techno ether. Ash's mind is totally blank. Relaxed. Eyes still closed, she slowly pulls out one of her earbuds and finds she can still faintly hear that fucking guitar playing downstairs. Fuck. The airport dream girl is floating behind her eyes. A cartoon, long pastel anime hair down to her feet, flicking around her knees flowing, obscuring and revealing a galaxy of secrets. Her airport dream girl hips, her ribs, up her back, her shoulders, down to her elbows, the palms of her hands, her throat, her beautiful chin, her nose, her ears, as she twirls, truth reflects off her like stars. She winks at Ash, an emoticon. Ash's mind is completely clear. She breathes deeply, feels nothing. She obsesses over the airport dream girl. Dream girl, dream girl, dream girl…

'Hey girl,' she hears. 'Are you in your own private cloud up here? May I join you?' Ash opens her eyes to see through the ash not Dick, not the girl from the airport, but some other guy standing beside her, arms folded. He's wearing a black hoodie with big white glyphs like xxx across the front, he's got spiked black hair, really baggy pants rolled just above the ankles. She thinks Green Day. He says, 'Do you ever feel like the MTV generation's inability to get up off the couch was a direct precursor to people like you and me secretly watching snuff on Xtube on our iPhones?'

Ash sits up. 'Who the fuck are you?' she says. 'Did Dick send you up here just to fuck with me?'

'Well, partially, I'm sure. Like, my dick sent me up here cos I needed a piss so I did that and that felt good, but then I noticed you were up here doing some suspended animation bullshit and that totally reminded me of how we're all going to die tonight, re: the end of the world. So I just wanted to check in, you know. Make sure you're alive. Which you are. And now that I know that you're not dead yet, I'm inviting you to come to a rave. Wait. Do you mean the guy, Dick?'

'Yes. The guy Dick. Not your penis. What's your fucking problem, dude?'

'Fuck Dick! That guy sucks! Wait, are you the uptight girl he took to the double Armageddon penetration manifestation feature at the drive-in just before?' He's thrusting his hips as he says that. 'He's been talking about you downstairs, like working it into his song. He said he almost got to score but a crazy guy was banging on the window just when he'd got you "sauced", whatever that means. That party downstairs sucks. Anahera's a cool person but I don't get why she lets guys like Dick into her life, let alone her apartment. Guys like Dick get so much airtime. I walked into that party and immediately wanted to press delete on the entire Auckland scene. I say end it all now if that's what life is. Fuck an acoustic guitar, I wish I had a gun. Dick's a wash-out, come party with me, I know what's up, girl. Did Dick make you pull a tarot card before he tried to fuck you? He's a fool. And I don't mean like The Fool card, which actually represents crazy wisdom. He's always trying to put on a show for international ladies, like, I'm assuming, yourself. Me on the other hand, I am totally pro-feminist, I'm also sensitive to lesbians and the broad spectrum of trans* identities. I'm a good ally. I'll be useful after the collapse.' He's down on his knees now, looking up at her, deep into her eyes. 'I know how to wear the same pair of boxer shorts five days in a row without making a mess. I'm a good kisser.'

Ash lies back again. 'I feel like I'm Tank Girl, in the future with no water, showering in talcum powder, living underground with a bunch of fucking kangaroos. I feel like I'm about to get sucked dry. You guys are *all* fools, and I'm stuck here.'

'But we are so far overground! You can trust me, I'm not a kangaroo. Look at the clouds, that's volcanic lavender. It's beautiful. I think it's going to storm. Dirty thunder. Do you want some Rescue Remedy? I've got Bach flower essences too. They say if you're prepared to take care of yourself for the first seventy-two hours of any incident, that's usually all you need to do. Someone will come find you then. And if you do decide to, I'll be there with you, washing dishes, making the bed.'

The relaxation track is still playing in one of Ash's ears, a dolphin call, a female voice telling her, 'We are now coming to the end of this relaxing session. Start to reanimate your body by wiggling your fingers and toes. And please make sure you are fully awake before engaging in your next activity.'

'What's our next activity?' Ash sits bolt upright.

'Believe and you will achieve, believe and it will be so, just stay true and never let go. Come with me to the year 2000. At the underground rave. Yep. I heard Skrillex is playing.' This boy is fucking crazy. He holds his hand out to Ash.

'Look dude, you just interrupted me halfway through a meditation. I need some time.' Ash just sits there. In a kind of foetal position. Then says, 'Okay, I feel like I'm in a movie, this feels stupid, scripted. There's something wrong.' The boy starts doing push-ups. Ash isn't sure she has come out of her relaxation session properly, she's monitoring all the sensations in her body. 'Also I want to eat something.'

'It's a beautiful night tonight. I'm so excited for the rave. My name is Mack, I'll be your host, your collapse partner. Will you be with me tonight?' He's holding out his hands. 'I wish I had a flower for you, you're pretty, what's your name, girl? You don't have asthma, do you? There's an asthma warning out.'

'Are you fucking with me, still?'

Mack grabs Ash's hands and swings her around. 'Let's remember this moment forever.' He takes a selfie with Ash and uploads it #nofilter. 'My feed is full of geeks making #nofilter jokes. Because of the ash. Do you get it?'

'Yeah, I got it. Thanks. I need to go back into the party downstairs to get my cousin Haydn.'

'Hey I think I know that guy! Tall, kinda nondescript-looking?'

'Yeah, that's Haydn. He's got kind of a sad face?' They're running down the building's stairs together.

'Yeah totally! Hey, I think my cousin Misty is like banging your cousin Haydn. Wait, if we're their cousins, does that make us related now?' He stops halfway down a flight of stairs. 'Like, would it count as incest if you and I hooked up?'

'Wait, no way! Haydn does not bang! And you need to do a trigger warning before you post that kind of shit around me. I'm calling bullshit on your "ally" status.'

When they get downstairs Anahera's apartment door is shut. The guitar playing has stopped. Ash tries the handle but it's locked and no one answers when Mack knocks. They go outside to peep through the window. In the living room they see figures snuggled up in purple satin sheets, watching an old bald alien with big blue eyes talking to them through the television. They bang on the window, but no one turns around to look.

ASH AND MACK WALK to the rave. Mack's pants are really low, he's holding onto the straps of his backpack and waddling. He says tonight, like every night, he'll be getting a natural high from yerba mate mixed with green tea, which he's got in a Nalgene drink bottle hanging off his belt. 'I put some blueberries in too,' he says. 'It's weird that free radicals are the bad ones, and that antioxidants are good.' He has Celtic tribal tattoos on both his triceps, a dragon tattooed over his ankle and he's doing chin-ups on everything, hanging street signs and bus shelters, like way too much energy. He has translucent blue plugs through his earlobes, he's talking about the first time he ever got in a fight. 'Some guy just walked up to me and smacked me right in the jaw, called me either "pussy faggot" or "PC faggot", or it could have been "pussy fascist".' Then he's talking about how he lost his virginity, 'I was fourteen and my lover was like, "are you attracted to me, physically?" because before that we'd only made out with no real touching and I said "yeah," because what else would I say? But honestly, I didn't experience any sexual urges or enjoyment at all until I was like nineteen-and-a-half but now, right now, I'm like sexually on ecstasy. I'm not afraid anymore.' He does a little jog, almost loses his pants. 'And now, we are almost at the rave.'

LASER LIGHTS AND LOW-FREQUENCY reverberations emanate from a four-storey warehouse, which from the outside does not appear to be structurally sound. Mack has no ID, and the security out the front doesn't believe he's over eighteen. They're barred and, walking away, Mack scowls, 'Fucking security at a squat rave? This is gonna be great.' But then he spots a gang of scally lads smoking, holding a door open around the side so Mack and Ash get in that way.

Inside the warehouse it's dark. Ash leans against a wall that feels wet, checking Facebook because she's got a notification of a message from Dick. It says 'hi from a guy you probably won't remember. ;)' Then she gets a bunch of texts, all at the same time, all from Dick's number. 'How r u going cuz? x Haydn,' and 'Hey where r u? x haydn' and 'Ash are you there? Did u go to rave? This is Haydn btw, write back soon please I want to see u badly' plus many more messages, all from Haydn, expressing varying degrees of desperation. Ash's phone must have gone out of range at some point.

Mack sits on a table. He looks at Ash while he dunks a tampon in his Nalgene bottle, sucks the liquid into his mouth, flicks it away. His jumper is off now and he's wearing a tight ENJOY COCK t-shirt. He has a clip in his hair. He's swinging his legs, yelling to Ash about once having snuck into a tropical island-themed indoor sauna and pool complex called Tropical Islands, open twenty-four hours every day in an old hangar, the biggest unsupported structure in the world. He talks like a fucking drill. Ash writes back to Haydn, 'I'm at a rave in a warehouse downtown, come meet me here!' Mack is lamenting the fact that a new generation of teenage activists will never understand that McDonald's is truly evil, they won't know the sexy McLibel struggle or understand that Nikes are made in sweatshops.

'McDonald's sell salads now,' he says, then, 'Psych!' He has Xs tattooed on his hands, not the classic big straightedge black ones, his are smaller and on his palms. Subtle, cute. They look home-done, a shaky curly cursive. He's holding that book *No Logo*. Not reading it, just holding onto it like it's part of his brand identity. 'I can feel it tonight. The rush, the love, the unity. I'm excited for the year 2000. I'm glad you're here with me. I'm not scared of Y2K. Are you?' He looks directly at Ash. 'I mean, are you still hungry?'

'Ya, so hungry. Can we please go get something to eat? Like, now?'

'Oh but Ashy, I have everything that you could ever need, right here.' Mack produces from his backpack a packet of Skittles, a bag of Spicy Sweet Chili Doritos, Oreos. 'They're all vegan, go silly on 'em!'

'Wow, this is so gross, I don't know what to say!' Ash rips open the Oreos. 'Hey Mack, why isn't there anyone else in here? Like, what's the deal? Where's the party?'

'Yes, I myself have been concerned with precisely this issue for some minutes now. I guess the rave must be somewhere else in here, should we go exploring?'

'Let's just head towards the pounding bass.'

Ash and Mack walk past a bunch of stainless-steel appliances, Ash munching Skittles. They're on an uneven concrete surface, dodging huge puddles on the floor. They go down a corridor that gets darker and darker and Mack's like, 'It's cool I've got my phone out,' but his phone won't turn on and neither will Ash's. They decide to keep walking, holding hands, each with one arm out in front because they can't just stay there in the dark and there's no point turning back. After walking super slowly for about twenty metres in absolute blackness, dark enough that Ash can't tell if her eyes are open or closed, and Mack is having flashbacks to his shit dad preaching on the horrors of death's kingdom, and Ash has to spit the Skittles out of her mouth because they taste so intense without colour, and Mack thinks that maybe this is the final solution—after all that, they turn a corner and see rainbow oscillating light illuminating a pile of bricks from behind a gap in the wall and the beat gets louder, louder.

BLUE-TINGED BERRY-SCENTED AIR. Huge oil-slick anodised marbles rotate on thick chains above heads like disco balls. One clue: rollerbladers everywhere. And almost everyone's wearing sunglasses. Swarms of partyographers burn flash traces into every raver's nightvision every few minutes. Mack shows Ash that under blacklight his eyes glow green and blue. 'They're patterned Earth balls,' he says. 'Like contact lenses, but they're not.' The DJ is a K-Pop star, wearing Nike Air More Uptempos and a t-shirt dress that says REAL IS A FEELING across the front. When someone snaps a photo she sticks out her tongue. A guy who looks like Angelina Jolie's boyfriend from that movie *Hackers*, the one who wears the soccer goalie top and has cropped maroon hair—the passive one—stands next to the DJ booth. Goalie shirts are the hottest soccer shirts.

'Does this feel to you like the rave scene from that Harmony Korine film?' Ash yells. 'I wish I knew someone who could get me drugs and show me which way to the bathroom orgy.' Everyone's teeth and freckles are glowing aqua. 'Just to watch, you know.'

'Yeah but maybe if we just go look for the bathroom we'll find the bathroom orgy.'

A girl walks past, she has a UV-reactive tattoo on her neck that says in a florid script something that looks like UNIVERSAL HEALTHCARE. Mack is looking at his phone. 'Americans have so much nervous energy,' says Björk in a Vimeo video autoplaying on the screen. 'Sick, my phone totally works again. Does yours?'

'Wait, what are we looking for again?' Ash asks.

'Bathroom orgy.'

Ash clicks her phone and tries the AirCon customer hotline. A cut-up voice tells her, 'AirCon customer support service is experiencing an increased volume of customer calls at this moment and the current wait time to speak with an operator is around four… teen… hours… and… twenty… six… minutes.' Ash hangs up.

On Mack's screen Björk's saying, 'It's just stupid to sing in Icelandic if people don't understand it.'

'Yeah my phone works,' Ash says. 'Let's go find the toilets.'

Mack and Ash follow a bunch of people down a passageway lined with ferns gaffer-taped to the walls, their roots still attached. Everything is damp and almost everyone is smoking. One girl is pointing to a dripping water pipe just above her head and saying, 'I hope this isn't poo water,' loudly, over and over again, but no one's listening to her. A partyographer snaps Mack and Ash, and Ash asks her where the bathroom is. The partyographer breathes hard and points further down the passageway. Then she scurries off in the other direction, casually snapping her camera at a girl with smoky eyes wearing deep-purple lipliner and a khaki Issey Miyake sleeveless shift dress who's popping the cork off a bottle of Cristal Brut.

When they get to the bathroom they're kind of shocked because there actually is an orgy going on in there. Mack is like, 'This shit always happens to me, it's called providence and it happens because I meditate everyday.' But he's also like 'Wow,' and bouncing around all the ravers deep-throating one another's pierced tongues. He watches closely until a guy with an X written in zinc on his cheek and a little puff of baby-blue hair slams him up against the wall and mechanically starts undoing Mack's baggy pants. 'Suck my UV see-through dick,' a girl yells to a leather daddy, who's next to Mack. She undoes her white PVC skirt and pulls out a citrus psytrance swirled strap-on dildo. Erect. Pulsing. Ribbed. A single drop of latex glistens down the front of her mini millennium bug t-shirt.

A cute boy standing near Ash says, 'This is like, amazing sexual exploration. They look like cornballs from Ponsonby on ecstasy, feeling the effectstacy. It's a spectacle, a real spectacle. Freaky behaviour in the club wilds.' He's wearing novelty glasses, googly eyes bouncing around on springs, a G-Shock watch, NASA t-shirt, baggy denim JNCO shorts and Osiris D3s that look pretty thrashed. He twirls his hair around his finger as he speaks. 'Everyone was scared before that some skinheads were going to turn up and beat the crap out of everyone, but then someone said that they all went down to Invercargill to beat up people at some other end of the world party, one that's legitimately at both the end and the edge of the world.'

Ash locks eyes with an orgy-girl in a fluoro yellow American Apparel dress who's sucking a lollypop while groping someone's ass and getting fingered. Mack bounces loose from the sexual scrum and says, 'Fuck! That sex is seething! So hot, like total Pompeii styles.' He looks at his phone. He's trying to bid on vegan Nikes on eBay, but his 3G has dropped out. 'Fuck! Why do the auctions always end in the middle of the night when I'm trying to party? I can't even deal.'

The guy by Ash with the eyes-on-springs glasses is still fumbling with his hair, like gazing into space. He turns to Mack, 'Hey, how do you think the International Date Line impacts on total global annihilation? Is that shit staggered, like explosions moving west, hour by hour over the course of the night?'

'Yeah, we die first!' says Mack. 'Aotearoa, number one!' But halfway through speaking Mack becomes properly aware of this other guy and his voice gets way softer, embarrassed, 'I mean, I guess…'

The guy gets up close to Mack, face to face, foreheads basically touching, and looks down at what Mack's doing on his phone, his spring-eyes bouncing all around.

'Hey, why are you bidding on sneakers when you know you're not going to wake up tomorrow morning? Silly rabbit.'

'What's your name?'

'Fidget.'

'You keep playing with your hair, Fidget. It's a cute quirk. I'm Mack. Don't ever stop.'

Rotating fans are positioned against the walls every couple of metres but the whole rave still feels muggy, totally airless. Fidget says, 'There are secret areas in this rave that are only accessible sometimes and no one's telling me who has the keys.'

A girl with beautiful hair that's a vertical gradient from ultraviolet to charcoal walks past and Mack points and says, 'Wow, who rolled all the Disney princesses into one?' Fidget is like, 'She's got TDK eyes. Is she Martian or what? She looks like a Froot Loop.' The girl is wearing a t-shirt that says IRL VS DREAMS. Mack starts rapping in her general direction: 'I roll with Disney princesses / this girl, like twenty-five amalgamated bad bitches wearing one glass slipper each / I am Flipper, you are Ariel, before she falls in love with an asshat and she can still speak fish / this girl is Jasmine riding hella magic carpet / through a desert sunset, she's Snow White virgin Apple / I'm a Mack Pro / forever dead iPhone battery girl / she's a strawberry swirl / I'm a Beast, her Prince Charming / Prince Florian I wanna get really really real / and Free Willy.'

The girl doesn't hear or doesn't care, just swishes away.

Fidget wanders over to a table with a little mountain of Tazos on it and Mack watches him go.

'You know what Mack?' says Ash. 'You think she's a Disney princess? But you will never ever get a girlfriend. I'm a girl so I know. You are hopeless and you're not a good ally.'

Mack responds in a drawl, 'Oh really, well guess what Ash? Guess what? I don't even want a girlfriend, I wanna boyfriend.' He's moving like he's hula-hooping but there's nothing around him. He looks back to Fidget, who's concentrating hard on the pile of Tazos on the table, like really locked in. 'You hear me Fidg? I wanna boyfriend. I wanna boyfriend who wears novelty glasses. I wanna fuck a boy who's a drug dealer and I wanna get a contact high every single night. I wanna listen to Kylie Minogue and spin around. I think I want to be with you.' He's snapping his fingers. 'Fidget? Fidget! Listen to me!'

'What? Hey, wassup Mack? I'm sorry I was… these Tazos. Wow. What were you saying?' Fidget is smiling. Like this :) He sticks his tongue out exacerbated, drug-fucked, scrunching his eyes. 'I'm tryna find all the holographic ones. I could give them to you. I think you'd like them, they're prettier, the colours jump right off them in the corners, the edges, see?' He hands Mack a *Pocahontas* Tazo, 'This one, the stars skip all around when you tilt it. It's homeopathic.' He's still smiling like this :)

There's a crew of dancers closeby. Dressed in identical black shirts and sweatpants, new-looking Nike Windrunners and armband patches that say HEAVEN'S GATE AWAY TEAM and when the DJ drops the beat on a hardstyle remix of Britney's 'Till the World Ends' they all start twerking, dancing fast but in slow-mo, one guy spinning on his back. When he pops up they all do a synchronised dance of death, slapping drinks out of people's hands, lots of retching and tumbling ticker-tape, performers bouncing everywhere, bursting balloons. One girl swings up and knocks a purple party disco-ball marble way off its axis and if this is supposed to be the end of the world, Ash is like, whatever, try harder. The track is ending, mixing into something by DJ Sammy or David Guetta, and all the dancers are falling to the floor, dead. But, like a weed-whacker, the dancers have parted the crowd to reveal a perfect girl, rainbow-lit, brain-lobe melting. Ash is obsessed.

'You guys, that's the girl from the airport,' she says, pointing beyond the gang of dancers. The boys don't hear, they're gazing at each other. 'You *guys*. I'm basically in love with that girl over there. I've been trying to manifest running into her again all day.' Ash is getting turned around by the crowd, the dancers are getting back up, apocalypse in retrograde. The girl is somewhere behind her and Ash is trying to use her phone's front camera to see her, but she's distracted by her own doughy face. Not enough sleep, she tugs her eyelid. 'I think that's her. Fuck, I need a shower. I need speed! I need to talk to this girl! *Fuck!* Do you guys understand me? We were both at the airport! At the same time! This morning! It's a major coincidence! And she's here now!' Ash is yelling, yanking on Mack's shoulder, but he's caught up watching Fidget build up an intricate tower of interlocking Tazos.

'Hey Fidget, Ash needs a Chupa Chup, an upper, whatever, help her out, she's tweaking.'

'Oh, here's a *Space Jam* one with sparkles.' Fidget slides another Tazo over to Mack, a strobe light half-speeds his actions. He puts his hand down his pants and pulls out a little drug baggie, 'And here's something for you Ashy, see now you swallow it, you'll be floating up in heaven with the angels, you'll be singing with Sammy Davis Jr.' Fidget is a total candyflip. His smile!

Ash swallows the pill with some of Mack's mixed-berry tea shit. She so desperately wants to talk to this girl, untouchable, completely unapproachable, so close but on another plane of consciousness, like freakishly attractive, a future step in human evolution without origin or reality moving purposefully through a dank rave-space, total cyborg, hyperreal, post-human, a body of light, no words… This girl, like a total monomaniac, walking towards Ash right now and like holy fuck, fuck, fuck, eye contact? No. She walks straight past Ash. Does not make eye contact.

'I should just go and talk to her. Introduce myself and just say "Hi." Okay, I'm gonna go do that.' Ash leaves Mack watching Fidget watching the Tazos. The airport dream girl is dancing by herself. She looks different though, like she's got drawn-on eyebrows now, and jewels on her face and shoes that make her even taller. She's dancing real lazy.

Ash strides across the room to the dance floor towards the girl. But before she's even close she's intercepted, a guy from the house party physically blocks her path, the one with green shit around his eyes. He's yelling, 'Ash! Ash!' She doesn't get why this guy knows her name or what he wants, she's trying to see the airport dream girl over his shoulder but the guy won't stop putting his face in front of her. She gives up and looks properly. 'Haydn? Oh wow, is that you?' The cousins embrace. Behind Haydn, Ash can see the girl with her hands behind her head, dancing in a circle of boys, mouthing the words to the song in slow motion. 'Wow, you grew up quick! You've been here what, four days and already you wear make-up?'

'Yeah except that this isn't make-up, or if it is I can't get it off. I've got a problem Ash. I met this girl, Misty, she sleeps a lot but she seems okay, and I really like her, but she was vomiting all day today. Vomiting Berocca, like really high vitamin C or B and,' the beat pounds loud, Ash is missing every other word, 'bright yellow and then orange, bile I guess, but then she touched me and we kissed on the mouth and it felt really good and fuck I am so in love with her. I put my knee between her legs and I kissed her hard but not deep,' Ash can't see the airport girl anywhere, 'and her tongue was going crazy in my mouth and I've never kissed like that before in my life but then it started to burn and I wanted to pull away but she said there was nothing wrong and I believed her and then we made love, and it felt like, fuck, so hard to believe, but then I got this other feeling so I pulled out because I thought I was going to nut and she was making this horrible noise and then I did nut, all over the sheets, but Ash,' Haydn is looking right into her eyes, 'when I came, my cum was green. Like, bright green.' His lip trembles. 'Like Gak.'

'Wait wait wait. Like, Nickelodeon Gak?'

'Yes. My ejaculate literally glowed in the dark!' His face crumples. 'And afterwards Misty wouldn't wake up, like, I could hear her breathing, I could feel her heartbeat, but I couldn't talk to her. I didn't know what to do. I went to talk to Dick and Anahera but they were asleep too and then I started walking here, I don't know, to find you.'

'Haydn, I don't know if this is the right time, but really, you need to use a condom.'

'I was using one! My cum just burnt straight through it, went all over the bed.' Haydn is crying.

On the other side of the room, a foreign hand hits the

table, toppling Fidget's Tazo tower. He covers his eyes in dismay, then looks up 'Hey, Bassy! You made it!' Unseen by Ash, her airport fantasy girl sits down on Fidget's lap. His chair breaks and they fall to the floor, rolling around on the ground and laughing, Bassy covering Fidget with kisses and hugs; peace, love, unity and respect.

Ash guides Haydn to the bathroom. 'Let's get your face cleaned up.' But when they get in there a guy with Björk buns is pushing two girls up against a wall, kissing both of them at the same time and touching their boobs. When Haydn sees this he kind of whimpers and turns away. Ash wets a wad of toilet paper and starts rubbing around his eyes. The line for the toilets is long and stupid and someone says, 'I think the best way to make somebody get a crush on you is by first pretending that you have a crush on them, then ignoring them completely.' Someone else bangs on each of the toilet doors in turn, yelling, 'C'mon, you've been in there for hours,' but the only response is two high-pitched giggles emanating from the one cubicle.

'Wow I wonder what this stuff is, it's totally not coming off.'

Haydn tries to joke like, 'I guess people show their true colours under blacklight,' but Ash doesn't smile. Haydn's still crying and she's rubbed his face so much that now it's kind of mottled purple. Or maybe her drugs have kicked in, because it's also kind of swirly? They go out to find Mack and Fidget again. Ash scans the dance floor to see if the airport girl is still around but she can't see her. When they get back to where the boys were a minute ago they're gone, instead a gang of Juggalettes in red face paint and strappy bikinis is sitting at their table playing Tazos in the dark.

Ash drags Haydn away and around a corner, where they

find Mack and Fidget in each other's arms. Sandwiched in between them is the airport dream girl, laughing hysterically. 'Oh my god it's starting,' Ash says to Haydn.

Mack is yelling at airport dream girl, like, 'You got five eyes!'

Fidget says, 'Nah but, she's got nine eyes including her actual eyes, and I'm seeing double so she's got eighteen and she's beautiful like an insect. I love her, Mack.' Above and below her eyes the airport dream girl has sparkly googly-eye stickers stuck onto her face, and a huge bloodshot eyeball bauble in her hair, it's actually kind of disturbing, hard to focus on which eyes are actually eyes. She presses on a baby-blue love heart that's stuck over her third-eye chakra, over and over again, protecting her from this cruel world. She seems flooded with love.

Everyone's got mad desires, dry mouths, abstract addictions—usually it's drugs but right now it's everywhere, everything, it's in the atmosphere.

The girl from the airport thinks Haydn is cute, says, 'I like your eyes,' bats her eyelashes. Then she notices Ash. 'Hey you're the girl from the airport. Hello. My name is Bassy and,' she holds out her hand for Ash to shake, 'I think we're going to be the best of friends.'

Bassy, Bassy, Bassy, what a beautiful name! Fuck! She's wearing Tommy Hilfiger wedges and she's like two feet taller than the boys. Mack whispers to Fidget, 'I love her, can we keep her?' and Bassy pretends not to hear but is visibly suppressing a grin.

An impromptu poetry reading is happening in the corner: shirtless gleaming men reading off their iPhones. Freaky cutie dancers in cages, boys with bad-attitude scowls wearing overalls done up over just one shoulder. All around are guys with waxy little dreads, septum rings, one guy is wearing an inflatable apple-green backpack, another wears white angel wings; every boy holds a glow stick.

'Hey where did all the girls go?' asks Ash.

'Twitter is Grindr,' says Fidget.

'I heard there's a princess room upstairs,' Bassy says, grabbing for Ash's hand. 'Let's go up there, I wanna fuck a mermaid. Like, do you reckon it's possible? C'mon, lemme get you a drink.' They climb the stairs.

'Bassy, I wanna ask you questions. Like, where are you from? I mean, I've never seen anyone like you.'

'Sure! I'm from here, from Auckland! I went to kindy with Fidget. I haven't been back in ages though. I don't like it here, too humid in summer. Weird things happen with this much water in the air.'

They stand in the doorway to the princess room. Ash and Bassy watch girls dancing around wearing tutus with side ponytails and heaps of balloons. There's a fog machine and giant inflatables. Five girls are screaming into the one microphone. Everyone is wearing big sunglasses, fluoro t-shirts, lots of Jeremy Scott for Adidas. A guy who possibly is Jeremy Scott is flanked by two girls who look Tumblr-famous, carrying big plush toys looking awkward, stoned. 2NE1 is playing on a stereo. A gang of boys in black hoodies and balaclavas spin umbrellas emblazoned with what might be second-wave feminist slogans, or maybe just super esoteric culture jams, around a girl headbanging on stage. Everything feels vaguely Occupy Wall Street. They're still only in the doorway; Ash doesn't want to go in. Bassy says her phone isn't getting any reception up here anyway so they go back to the staircase.

'Hey Bassy, at the airport, what were the border guards scanning on your arm?'

'Implanon.'

'Like WTF, why is your biometric data contained in your contraceptive implant?'

'Oh don't be a dummy, girl. Your data is contained in everything you own and do. Believe in NSA, girl. Never Say Anything. Be one girl with two names—two boyfriends, two bank accounts, two passports. Better yet, be one girl and one boy at the same time. I've never looked back.'

Way below, Mack is still trying to bid on those Nikes

that are about to end on eBay but he can't connect to the internet. 'The only good thing about living in the Southern Hemisphere is that I thought I wouldn't die when the world ends, because this hemisphere is so much smaller than the other one,' he says. 'I thought we'd be safer in the backwards backwoods nowhere.'

Bassy and Ash sit together halfway down the stairs but Bassy's phone still won't work properly. Bassy leans towards Ash, puts a hand on her thigh, says, 'Eminem has this song called "Superman" which is really smart and so misogynistic.' Her eyes are glowing. 'It's about a silly girl who thinks she knows Marshall Mathers III just because she knows his rap persona Slim Shady. The song is smart because Eminem is always playing a character, he's a parody of himself. He slaps that woman off her barstool!' Bassy giggles. 'Misogyny is powerful and that's why I like it.'

Metres away, but in another universe, Fidget says to Mack, 'You are my Rosetta Stone and now I can understand everything.' They're nuzzling, dancing real close.

Some dude strolls past and laughs. 'Your stupid glasses are your Rosetta Stone, fascist.' He stands over Mack and Fidget, says, 'What are you dudes, bisexuals?' but they hardly notice him.

'This earthquake needs more zing, baby, like, why aren't we getting an evacuation order yet? Not even an exclusion zone? Hey, Fidget, I think I love you,' Mack says.

'Hey bozo, it's not an earthquake, it's a volcanic eruption.' This guy starts pushing Mack. 'I'm the kind of dude who pulls knives at parties and can listen to babies cry for hours without feeling the need to do anything. You guys better watch out. I don't even brush my teeth.' Then he moonwalks away, over to his friend who high fives him.

Bassy is whispering in Ash's ear, 'I need to tell you something important before I fall asleep.' LMFAO's 'Party Rock Anthem' starts playing and Bassy and Ash look at each other and Ash's mind goes totally blank, Bassy is so perfect. By the time she thinks to ask her what she was going to say, Bassy is walking away from her, down the stairs, her hands clamped over her ears.

Ash and Bassy find Fidget and Mack on the dance floor and Haydn lurking in a shadow nearby. They all separately affirm that they can't get online on their personal devices, so like, what's the point of even being at the rave? They all go to leave, but the exit is blocked by a guy wearing a bucket hat telling everyone that there are cops outside so he's not allowed to let anyone in or out. There's a wasted guy swinging from a pipe above them who looks like he's going to crack his skull when he falls. The exits are crammed and when Haydn wonders aloud if there is a paramedic on site, no one responds. They keep standing by the doorway, Bassy pleading with the guy in the bucket hat. 'We need to use the internet! Please let us out before the world ends! I need to see my baby sister one last time.' After approximately ten minutes of pleading, bribery and either fake or real crying, he finally agrees. 'There's no way you're getting back in though. And don't blame me if you get arrested, shit is fucked up out there.'

Haydn tells Ash that he wants to go back to Anahera's to check on Misty and Ash says, 'Don't let Mack know.' They walk ahead a bit. Haydn bows his head and starts crying again. 'I just feel really bad... I need to see...' He says he'll call Ash when he's back at Anahera's and starts walking faster than the rest of the group.

'Okay but wait, Haydn,' Ash yell-whispers, 'did you hear

what Bassy said to me? She totally remembered me from the airport!' Haydn looks confused. 'She noticed me! She must feel the exact same way about me as I feel about her, like we must have both been totally obsessing over each other all day. I feel so nice, this really makes my day! Night! Good luck with Misty! Star-cross'd lovers all round.' She does a peace sign with her fingers. Haydn scoots.

A couple of metres back, Bassy is telling Fidget, 'I tried to add that girl Ash just before but then I saw that we don't have any mutual friends.' She's whispering. 'Fidget, this is so weird. Isn't the current protocol "avoid friending people with whom you have no mutuals"?'

'Chill Bassy, that's just if you haven't met them in the flesh because they might be a spybot or a cop. But this, this may be true love! This is like what old people must have experienced when they had anonymous sex with strangers. It's like when all that existed was what was physically around, no static, no updates. Meeting someone with no mutuals is rare, it's special, relish it Bassy. You are lucky.'

OUTSIDE IS AS HUMID and sweaty as inside was. Their ears are ringing. A ferris wheel on the waterfront had its steel melted on the first hot day of summer and since then construction crews have been up there day and night working under huge spotlights. But no one can tell if they're still deconstructing the old metal form or if they're reconstructing a new one, stronger, built for climate change. No matter how long they work, it always looks the same. But tonight, instead of construction workers, there are munters up there. Base jumpers and people with bungee cords just fucking around, no one's actually jumping. They've got balloons and streamers and vuvuzelas, confetti. Mack points to the horizon, to the volcanic plume with jabs of lightning emanating from it, still distinct through the red haze all around them. He takes an iPhone photo. 'See? Dirty thunder.' The photo is blurry.

Around the city, people are setting off firecrackers like it's New Year's, shooting BB guns, eating McDonald's, cartwheeling and screaming, stomping over parked cars. Helicopters fly overhead, shining beams of light that illuminate men pissing against buildings, women staggering around on broken heels, ankles. Shady dudes lurk down the street from the rave selling water, flashlights, batteries at exorbitant prices, luxury handbags and perfumes relatively cheaply. They're keeping their wares away from the cops who are parked outside the rave, lights flashing, but for once it doesn't seem like they're fighting tonight, just doing damage control. One cop is just staring straight up, into the sky. An elderly woman, wearing one of those white medical face masks that are popular in Japan, implores the rave fallout victims to cover their mouths. 'Active volcanoes emit toxic fumes, keep your face covered!' Next to her a sad clown clutches a wicker basket filled with fake red roses, the heads of which flash on and off like bike lights. 'Make tonight last, buy one for your girlfriend,' he winks at Fidget.

Mack walks up to the window of Farmers department store and fly kicks the glass. It doesn't break. An alarm goes off. A man wearing a sandwich board that says THE END IS NEAR appears and slaps Mack with a pamphlet that says SINBUSTERS. He tells him to repent or go to hell, splashing water in his face. Mack whines, sulking hard, 'I wanna go to hell though.'

As I walk, I write a eulogy for her in my mind. 'When Misty was confident, she was a total lioness, but when she wasn't she just froze, fell apart. She constantly needed to have like twelve things to do, she needed love and attention all of the time.' I'll have to find out her birth date. I wonder how old she is. I miss her. I wonder what her last name was… is?

'She sang pretty. So pretty but so cheesy, the kinds of songs I ordinarily would have rolled my eyes at people playing, like Radiohead, like Jeff Buckley, like a backpacker. But when she did it, she did it right, made those songs truly sing again. But now only a couple of hours later I can only hear a few muffled tones in the back of my mind. Fuck drugs, this girl was pure love and I'll never forget her and I need her. Rest in peace Misty No-last-name.' I hope she is still alive.

When I get there, Anahera's apartment feels so intense, so moist, abandoned. Misty isn't there. I check everywhere, all around the property, and then I go up to the roof because that would be the best scenario, Misty up there scratching HADYN into the bench. She'd look like shit, her hair matted, her eyes bloodshot, but I'd love her even more for it.

'I put Rohypnol in the punch,' she'd say to me. 'I thought it would be cool for everyone to go to sleep, you know? Just for the night. For the end of the world. I like your eyes like that, you look fucked as hell, bad. Do you think I can just puke off the side of this building?' And the Earth would turn and the sun would rise again and Dick's phone would start ringing and we would get another chance at life, together.

MACK PUSHES THE UP button on an elevator. He asks Fidget, 'Did you ever see that movie *Mallrats*?'

'Of course. Did you ever read that book *Fifty Shades of Grey*?'

'No fucking way. Did you ever watch that movie *Kids*?'

'Yes, every night before I go to sleep, doesn't everyone?'

Upstairs, this internet café is packed, it's actually like a wilder scene than the rave was. Better lighting too. A man who either looks like, or is, Kim Dotcom sits near the entrance looking bored, off-colour, like he needs some sunlight.

Bassy whispers to Fidget, 'I need coins for internet? Can't we go surf at McDonald's for free?' Mack starts fuming, he gets out *No Logo* again and slumps around reading it aggressively. Then he glares over the pages pointedly and whispers 'McFuckingMurderer' at Bassy while running his thumbnail across the front of his neck. In an open tab Bassy watches a realtime projection of the ash spinning around the Southern Hemisphere, the same one Ash saw on the *Guardian* site at the airport. It's majorly dense now, mega purple. Bassy logs into Skype.

There are cool fashion hacker girls at the internet café, and loser hacker men too. The twelve-year-old webmaster of a blog called FAsH1ON HA¢K£Rs is trying to explain 'hacker fashion' as it is portrayed in popular culture and magazines to an actual loser hacker who keeps yelling, 'Like what the fuck is a "hacker" look?' She is patiently explaining, 'Well, it's basically like motocross pants, a Quicksilver rash vest, silver eye make-up, complicated boots, technical sunglasses. Maybe blue hair dye too. But I can't argue with you because you are a real hacker and you are wearing your school leaver's jumper from 1994, so that's a thing too. But in popular culture hacking is framed as a very fashionable subculture, futuristic, often sexy.'

Mack buys a Jolt Cola from the guy behind the counter. At some point in the night he's noticed that Fidget says 'dada' instead of 'data'. There's a man in the corner explaining the intricacies of hacking handcuffs using shareware and 3D-printed keys. The FAsH1ON HA¢K£Rs blogmaster rolls her eyes, says 'Spare me.'

Mack tweets, 'Some more cool acronyms: FTW, WTC, 911.'

Bassy receives a call, on Skype, from her little sister LaCie.

A group of teenage girls sit near the window, QR code temporary tattoos stuck around their mouths so that when you look at them through this app they made themselves they're blowing AR kisses, Fiorucci angels, stars, love hearts and teddy bears, seahorses, whatever, floating up and around, away from their mouths. Their sharp eyebrows are flocks of lightning that move around and storm when these girls get moody. One girl wears a t-shirt that says I HACKED YOUR BOYFRIEND and a gross hacker dude is trying to pick her up even though she looks, like, eleven years old. SIM card nails. Nails with flip-down sunglasses. Lemonade Love & Hope nails. Fashion club styles that appear to be trending tonight are cotton singlets and boxer shorts printed with patterns from cartoons, strong slumber-party vibe, a million friendship bracelets, backwards snapbacks, eyemasks worn high on foreheads like headbands. And swelling à la Orlan, Walter Van Beirendonck, Nicki Minaj, Amanda Lepore, Amanda Bynes, Patrik Söderstam. One fashion club girl has Leigh Bowery's one big leg, plus crazy knee and elbow pads, plus the thickest coke-bottle glasses and a Snoopy band-aid across the bridge of her nose. She is taking a vote to see who wants to coedit a Disney Adventures aesthetic publication that is just pictures ripped from Tumblr with text written while on tranquilisers.

The computers at the internet café seem way older than they need to be. Maybe it's more secure that way for the l33t hackers, maybe it keeps out anyone who would just want to skim the surface.

There's a diagram on the wall explaining how this café stores up internet connectivity. Ash is looking at it trying to understand how it works. Surely you can't save up a live fibre-optic connection? The sign shows a few graphs, a map, and an illustration of a submarine cable burning fluoro red along the bottom of an oceanscape with cheeky-looking tropical fish and dolphins frolicking around it, grinning and doing thumbs up, coral shaped like smileys and stars, and along the bottom it says, 'When the time comes, the internet will shut off gradually, not all at once.' Small print along the bottom claims that even after a theoretical New Zealand–wide network crash, this café will continue to provide high-speed internet to the public for up to three hours. Ash wonders if this is already happening, the internet shutdown, because everyone's phones stopped displaying 3G almost an hour ago. No one has any kind of phone signal anymore.

Bassy's little sister LaCie is in Dubai. Via Skype her hair looks high-gloss blonde violet, in braids. She's talking about being friends with Suri Cruise. Their mother walks past the screen and is like, 'Hi Bassy, how are you? I can never keep LaCie's friends straight. One minute she's skyping with Suri, the next she is talking to Siri on her iPhone.'

'Suri is Tom Cruise's daughter. She's an eight-year-old Scientologist. She's your own daughter's best friend, even I know that and I haven't lived with you guys for like a million years.'

'Nicole Kidman mothered a child? That doesn't seem plausible!'

'No, well actually yes Mum, but Tom and Nicole broke up over ten years ago. Suri's mother is the actor who played Dawson's best friend on that TV show, *Dawson's Creek*.'

'Well I never. It's on the tip of my tongue… you mean Pacey?'

'No mum, Joey. The girl character.'

Bassy and Ash hear the shutter sound of LaCie taking screencaps on the other end. Bassy says to Ash, 'Hey check this out.' She tabs over to lacierugged.tumblr.com and there are like forty-five screen-caps of Bassy and Ash, already, with captions like, 'my cool big sister and her cool girlfriend', but they're spread out amongst other posts, including a runway shot of an Ashish model wearing an iridescent sequined top inscribed with the slogan SAY NO TO DRUGS but the O in NO is a fat yellow winky; a group shot of a girl gang from Harajuku called The Birds of Paradise; a 'save the slow loris' video with like a million notes and comments from conflicted tweens who think taking animals from the wild, ripping out their teeth and keeping them in cages is wrong but 'they r just soooo kute!' So judging by LaCie's Tumblr she's been really busy, but on Skype she's totally hands-free and at one point during the conversation she grabs for and starts drinking a blueberry and kale milkshake but the posts just keep coming. LaCie explains to her big sister, 'All those posts are queued, but I guess you wouldn't understand what that means. I wrote a script so that when I take a screenshot it automatically uploads to my Tumblr. I want my followers to see what I'm seeing, and what I'm seeing is my computer screen.' As she says 'computer screen' she does a body roll and her computer makes the shutter sound again five times in quick succession.

'Hey what is that t-shirt LaCie? It looks cool.'

'Well, our teacher said we don't know what is going to happen from now on, so she gave out these t-shirts. She gave one to each of us just in case. Look at the back.' She swivels around in her computer chair. On the back, LaCie's t-shirt says in a ye olde English font, NVR EVA BEEN 2 A RAVE B4.

'Wow, LaCie, what's that about?'

'My teacher said that if there is something like a Pompeii that happens to us here, it will be cool for the people who find us to know that raving is an activity for people a bit older than someone my age. To go down in history as a Rave Verizon.'

'Did your teacher say Verizon, or virgin?'

'I don't know, Bassy. Hey, wait, Suri is on the other line I want to chat to her, okay? Bye.' She hangs up.

Some guys in the café are wearing gas masks, they reckon due to the ash in the air, but it looks more like cosplay and one guy is talking conspiracy theory stuff.

At some point there is a blackout and a *Mad Max*–style girl wearing a leather jacket over a t-shirt that says FUCK GOOGLE, ASK ME takes charge. She's wearing patchy punk pants and a silver mask obscuring the entire left-hand side of her face, and she gets all up in the server stack with pliers, her booted leg slammed up against the wall, tugging at shit, trying to restore the connection. Someone says, 'Losing all your data for the first time, you're fucked now,' to someone else who's just dropped their external hard drive on the floor. 'Good luck trusting anything not in the cloud for the next couple of years, mate. Actually, the way we're going good luck trusting anything *in* the cloud too.' He chuckles. The internet at the internet café is faltering. Failing? Slow downloads corrupt.

Mack is rolling around on an office chair and Fidget is straddling him, pretty awkwardly in super baggy jean shorts, singing an acappella medley of the songs 'I Can't Help Falling in Love,' 'Fool in Love' and 'Lovefool'.

Time alone is precious. At some point the Kim Dotcom guy disappears but Bassy is the only one who notices. For every girl who is half-alive, delayed, grounded with no place to sleep, Bassy takes a nap on Fidget's shoulder.

A fourteen-year-old girl from the fashion crew starts talking in an accent about Ragnarök. A series of future events, including a battle, foretold to ultimately result in the death of a number of major figures including heaps of Nordic gods, the occurrence of various natural disasters, and the subsequent submersion of the world in water. She's relating it to the end of the world as imagined tonight, in the midst of the volcano ash outside, and with the Mayan calendar thing. She's a great storyteller, lots of suspense, until someone points out that she's furtively reading off Wikipedia on her iPhone under the table. 'Legend has it that afterwards, the world will resurface anew and fertile, the surviving and reborn gods will meet, and the world will be repopulated by only two human survivors.'

'Shotgun being one of the survivors,' shouts Mack. 'I know how to wear the same pair of boxers for five days in a row without making a mess and I'm a good kisser.'

Ash is holding up crystals saying a chant. 'Lucky charms to type on my iPhone, no harm to come to my loved ones.' She looks in turn at Mack and then Fidget and then Bassy.

Bassy wakes up from her nap, squeals, 'What are you looking at?'

'I was just surfing the internet,' Ash says.

'Yeah, well, so was I. But you know what, not having a boyfriend just because you're waiting for Ryan Gosling to save you from stepping in front of a taxi because you're jetlagged, that's stupid because yeah these things do happen, but you can't count on them happening to you. I used to date the vegetarian guy from The Pirate Bay but I dumped him. I say go hard or go home.'

'I can't. You can't either. In this instance we cannot exceed our physical bounds. We still need to eat, we're still stuck in Auckland. I'm not waiting for Ryan Gosling, I'm totally obsessed with you. You are like a golden beam to me. I feel so real with you.'

'Oh really? Because I just feel kind of flat when I'm around you,' Bassy replies. 'No offence.'

The internet is now officially down at the internet café.

The *Mad Max* girl yells, 'Alright, everybody out, nothing left to see here. Everybody go home, go enjoy the end of the world in the comfort and safety of your webless hellhole.'

Someone outside yells, 'I'm on Saturn! How am I still breathing!'

'Hey Fidget can I crash at yours tonight?' Bassy asks.

'You could, except I don't have any place. I thought maybe we could stay at Mack's?'

'Sorry guys, I'm living totally home-free at the moment. Hey Ash, didn't they hook you up with a hotel because your flight got grounded?'

'I don't know, I didn't stick around the airport long enough to find out.'

'It's okay, don't worry, I know a place we can stay,' Bassy says.

They go outside. 'Where are all the cars?' asks Mack. 'Ever see that movie *28 Days Later*?' But on the other hand maybe Auckland just feels like a chill place, like conceivably no one would be up early on the Saturday before Xmas. A neutral disaster with nu-rave effects, but when will it wear off, wear down? Maybe there are no cars out because no one is awake at five in the fucking morning.

'Wait, where did Haydn go?' asks Fidget.

THE WAY YOU FEEL silly and crusty when you've spent the night awake with your new crush and you don't ever want it to end and you don't know what will happen next.

'Fuck!' Ash says. 'I think my bags are still in Dick's truck.' She tries calling his mobile. 'Fuck, no reception! This network sucks! We are fucked! Fuck! I keep forgetting. No reception ever again.' Bassy is just shaking her damn head. Ash remembers the weird Facebook message she got from Dick a few hours earlier.

The sky is misty, foggy. Ash, Bassy, Mack and Fidget keep walking up through the city and over a big hill. They look back down to the city and they see automated light sequences but there are no cars left to stop for them, red and green lights blinking for no reason.

After a few minutes a single car zooms past.

Ash is worried they'll get hit hitchhiking in the mist and ash before dawn, which feels stupid since there aren't any cars, but somehow this makes it feel more likely that if a car does go past it will run them over. Mack has one thumb out and the other through his belt loop, doing a lopsided scowl like a cowboy psycho. Ash doubts anyone will pick up a pack of rave casualties munting on the side of the road.

She wants to get a cab but Bassy says, 'Okay, Ash, but you're a coward if you don't try more things.' Ash is like panicking and speechless, like so overwrought, but then Bassy says sorry for the girl-hate and that she just knows there won't be any taxis available right now, maybe ever again.

Mack and Fidget walk further up the road, so Ash sticks out her thumb too. 'Actually maybe let's hide over here,' Bassy says, dragging Ash behind a bush. 'The kind of driver who would pick up two guys might be less predatory than the kind of driver who would pick up two girls, marginally.' Bassy is calling Fidget and Mack 'Beavis and Butthead' behind their backs; the two of them are acting silly fools on the side of the highway.

'They might find our bones and plug in our phones and see who we were. Or who we thought we were,' Fidget says to Mack, his thumb out.

Ash is trying not to look at Bassy. She hears a car coming and pokes her head up. 'Shit! I think it's Dick's car! This is the best luck ever! This is Mack's providence!'

'No fucking way,' says Bassy, 'am I ever getting in a car with that guy. Never. Again.'

'Look, I've noticed this Dick guy cops a lot of flak, but I think generally he's just a regular good guy.' Ash is lying to herself, and she's lying to Bassy, the only person who matters to her in this moment. Sometimes you just want your bags back really badly.

'He's not a good guy, Ash. If you've met him you should know that. I'm not getting in his car.'

'Hey Ash, Bassy,' yells Mack from the road. 'Are you guys coming?'

'Go without me,' Bassy tells Ash.

'We can't! We don't even know where we're going without you. I need you. I'm obsessed with you. Please! It's probably not Dick, let's just go out there and have a look.' Ash physically pulls Bassy towards the pig hunter... and it's totally not Dick driving.

'Jesus! Where did you girls pop up from?' says the old lady driving the car. Fidget and Mack are already sitting in the back, in the ute tray. Bassy reluctantly gets into the front of the car after Ash and they roll off, away. Bassy whispers to her, 'Like I said, I just feel kind of flat when I'm around you. I'm really sorry. I'm not great with relationships. I think I'm better just loving myself. I don't know how to touch.'

'Hello I'm Sylvia and I'm a pig hunter.'

'Thanks for picking us up, Sylvia, we haven't seen many cars around this morning. Thank you for stopping for us.'

Bassy is still whispering only just loud enough for Ash to hear. 'The first time I went to a therapist, when I was twelve, I thought "finally". I'm totally fucked up. I used to check MySpace, refresh fifteen, twenty times in a row, not wanting to, actively thinking "I don't want to look at MySpace" while typing myspace.com into the address bar. So disappointed in myself. My therapist told me to wear this bracelet on my right arm and when I was participating in self-harm I had to move it to my left arm...'

'So where are you young'uns heading?' Sylvia asks.

'Bassy, do you know?'

Bassy yells 'No,' then says under her breath, 'Unfortunately, my therapist never told me when I could safely move it back to my right arm so it just sits here on my left arm, most hours of most days, reminding me of just how much I hate myself.'

'I guess we're just escaping the inevitable end of the world,' says Ash.

Sylvia says, 'But darling, you know that the world isn't actually ending, don't you? It's just racist folk who believe that shit, all this because a new cycle of the Mayan calendar is starting! This is an exciting time! You're racist if you think the world is going to end.'

'But the volcano! The fumes!'

'Yeah well, see, that's why I'm getting out of the city. Good thing you're coming with me. Most everyone else has left already. Smart folk.'

'I think Dick has a photo of you up in his car,' Ash whispers to Bassy.

'That is so sick.'

'He told me he made an app with some girl, who sold it to Tom from MySpace—is that you? He said you have a girlfriend, a princess?'

'That's an untrue rumour,' says Bassy.

'Isn't that tautology?' whispers Ash.

'No, because there can be true rumours, but this one is untrue. It's an untrue rumour. Nuclear acid.'

'You girls aren't much company, I should have got those boys riding up front. It's rude to whisper, don't you know?' Sylvia sticks her hand out the window and bangs on the roof of the car. Fidget and Mack bang back. Ash and Bassy sit in the pig hunter without speaking.

About an hour later Sylvia drops them off by the side of the highway, drives on. Bassy directs everyone to walk down a beautiful country road that leads away from the highway. The wind is violent, it whips them around, but it's warm. A soft dawn is beginning to glow on the horizon. Fairy floss ash clouds, even an hour away from Auckland, diffuse low light. Ash is thinking like it's an indie photoshoot, imagining cameras, Diana lomos, rainbow diffraction. A two-page spread, horses in a field next to where they walk, a kaleidoscope filter. Pastel-coloured hair, a warm wind, chiffon. December. Desolation. Fruit trees and flowers and hummingbirds, bumblebees, Bassy and Fidget fill Mack's backpack with feijoas. It feels so Studio Ghibli. They walk past a cemetery. Everything is real, vibrating. Delphiniums grow through gaps, they all wish on a dandelion. The haze in the air, glowing yellow and pink, light interference dust. Bassy holds a flower up to Ash's chin and says, 'Do you like butter? This soursob says you do.'

A giggle, 'We're so healthy, rosy-cheeked, it's unreal, cos we're also so fucked up. Coming down, sleep-starved.' Four angels, saints, the Spice Girls after Ginger left.

'Just imagine driving a coastal road in California along the edge of a cliff and next to the beach, top down, an Hermès headscarf over your perfect hair, huge Didion sunglasses, a soft golden bracelet glinting on your tan arm in the sun,' Fidget says.

Bassy's holding a rifle now, a big stick, leaning on it like a trekking pole as she walks. Ash asks Bassy if her life has always been this way, spectral, shrouded in diffuse light, Blundstones on a dirt track, kicking up dust.

Mack turns to Ash. 'Hey Ash, stay with me tonight.' Wistful, playful, reminiscing after only hours. He's picking flowers. He and Fidget touch fingertips, laugh, kick rocks, make out. Every child in every airport wears light-up shoes. Bassy whips her hair back and forth, mercurial, shifting. She laughs. The sun rises all around them, takes its sweet time.

Colours off the fucking spectrum.

At one time or another, everyone experiences periods so crazy they forget important elements completely until they read back through their diary from that time and place, and even then they feel unsure about what was real, what they fabricated in the telling, even though it's not in their nature to make shit up. Walking deeper and deeper into the countryside. There are tracks made by goats but no animals around. 'We didn't plan this out at all.'

Fidget's G-Shock bleeps. 'Damn, solstice! Guess what? We're still alive!'

A world without air travel. Mack and Bassy are ideating all the things that they are going to need after the collapse. Bassy thinks of gold, but Mack is like, 'Okay princess, what are you going to do with a shiny bit of metal? We need seeds and guns.'

'This is such a joke. We end up out in the country and it's maybe the end of the world, but we'll never know what happened because there's no reception and my phone battery is almost dead. I guess the city is just boring, normal. When we're out here nothing exists and we can pretend,' Fidget says. 'Imagine no internet.'

'But I don't like walking in the long grass,' says Ash. 'I'm afraid of snakes.'

'There are no snakes in New Zealand,' Bassy, Fidget and Mack say in unison.

They arrive at the gates of a mansion in the middle of a field. Bassy shakes the gates and, since they don't budge, she starts climbing one. Her broken Tommy Hilfiger wedges hang off her ankles on ribbons as she grabs at the iron gates with her grubby toes.

Ash is like, 'Do you know the people who live here?'
'Yeah, who lives here?'
'Who cares?'
'It's my uncle's house.'
'It looks pretty abandoned, where's your uncle?'
'He's imaginary. Look, Ash, I'm pretty tired.'

Mack is like, 'I'm gonna draw on the walls. And then I'm gonna go get Misty from the city and she's gonna colour them in.'

'Hey Mack, Haydn couldn't wake Misty up last night but, like, that doesn't necessarily mean anything. Like, I hope she's okay.'

'What?'

'She was breathing, he could feel her heartbeat. Don't stress. She's okay.'

Lupins grow everywhere, through the floorboards, a house more outside than in. Fields of blue and purple flowers. 'Do we all have to take up handcrafts like sewing and hunting to survive until someone finds us? In one hundred years?'

Ash asks Bassy, 'What did you want to tell me? Before LMFAO. At the rave, what did you have to tell me?'

'It doesn't matter anymore.'

'Are we out here just for now, or forever? It can't take us that long to get back to the city,' says Fidget. 'I feel empty.'

'If we're going to be back-to-the-landers, I want to make babies,' says Mack.

'I can't make babies,' says Bassy.

'Don't look at me,' says Ash.

'Fidget, will you make babies with me?' Mack asks.

'I can't make babies yet,' says Fidget, 'I never got my first period.' Ash slaps at a fly on her shoulder.

Bassy says, 'Well, we've got violets, a firepit, some weeds—we could try to smoke them, make an apple bong—a swimming pool, that stagnant dam at least, we're Calvin Klein models, luxuriance by the pool. A party for life. You, and you, and you, and me.'

Ash says, 'I don't even need my computer anymore. What am I going to do, look through my Photo Booth photos? I don't even want it anymore.'

Bassy takes off her shoes and her top and she has a tattoo like Rihanna's down the side of her torso that says 'Just let go and don't bother the future'. A girl thing, a girly tattoo.

For a moment there's a steep rise in temperature and a loud swoosh across the landscape. Infrared sauna, but nothing happens, no one dies.

Mack's like, 'We don't have anything we need. How are we going to look after ourselves? We need seeds, and vitamins and clean water, and guns and batteries, and a torch and you guys are gonna need bananas for the comedown just today and we need to know how to fight, and how to kill animals, and we need pharmaceuticals. And Wellington boots. Let's just relax hey guys?'

Fidget's like, 'We do have some pharms, like about twenty-three mollys down my pants. And I think a whole sheet of acid in my shoe.' Energy flash.

'We're basically living the movies,' says Bassy. '*The Beach*, *28 Days Later*, *Melancholia*, *2012*. All of them. But no zombies.'

'I wish the Notes app for iPhone was more stable,' says Ash. 'Like, I don't even have a piece of paper. I'm going to forget my entire personal history in about five minutes. What do we do, just sit on our phones trying to take everything in until the batteries are completely drained and then just hope that one day we'll have internet again, electricity maybe? We don't even have a charger.'

Flowers fall in slow motion, birds drop from an ashy sky.

'You know, I feel comfortable with you guys, but I really need a drink of water,' says Ash. 'I'm thirsty.'

Mack starts tattooing 'the world is sick so kiss me quick' down his forearm in biro ink, fast. He uses the hem of his t-shirt to get excess ink off himself, but every time he does it just spreads further. Up his fingers, onto the heel of his hand, all down the front of his pants. He spits on his arm.

Fidget says, 'When you're done doing that, don't pick at it.'

ACKNOWLEDGEMENTS

Excerpt from *Auteur at The End of the Earth* by Briohny Doyle published with permission from the author. Fashion hackers' make-up inspired by Thea Baumann/Metaverse Makeovers. Thanks to Matthew Linde for giving me that description of Bless No. 38 iPhone 4 cover. Regrette Etcetera told me about the McKenna brothers like five years ago. The bit in which Ash is on the roof doing a meditation was first published in issue one of *Magasine*. Thanks to Sarah Harrison and Katherine Botten for your reading and support. Thank you Katie Collins, Victoria Anne Reis, Samuel Shanahoy, Rina Anxiety, Gwyn Porter, Sophie Soni, Vincent Silk, Celeste Aldahn, Christopher LG Hill, Ashlin Raymond, Agatha Kowalewski, Oliver van der Lugt. Thanks Claire Mahoney for letting me know which other volcanoes are visible from the summit of Mt Eden. Thank you to PB PR, Pauline, Amalia Ulman and Clara Chon for lending me your works for presentation in *Not Dreams*. Build up to rave generated while listening to UNICORN KID TOKYO 1999 SUPERSUPER MIXTAPE on repeat, Le1f mixtapes, Fatima al Qadiri. In the last month of writing *No Limit* I read one essay from Eileen Myles' *The Importance of Being Iceland* every morning before writing, watched every Björk documentary I could find, listened to M.I.A. and Kt Spit on repeat. Thank you Johannes Jakob. I may be forgetting someone/something.

ALSO FROM HOLOGRAM

The Loud Earth
Elisabeth Murray
(May 2014)

'Deeply unsettling, Murray's prose is luminous.' Romy Ash

A recluse lives in a mountain cabin above a lakeside tourist town. Acquitted of the brutal murder of her parents, she remains guilty in the eyes of the town. Shut away from their fear and anger, her world is reduced to the landscape around her: the mist across the mountains, the sway of bayonet grass, the clear cry of a falcon. And above all the lake—its colours and rhythms, the answers it seems to hold.

But one night a young woman arrives on her porch. A stranger to the town, Hannah doesn't know the stories told about this outcast. A romance blossoms. But the recluse's violent past won't stay buried, Hannah unearths memories of shadows and blood. Amid dark cellars and crisp ski runs, rushing water in grottoes and whiskey by firelight, a call rises from the deep of the lake.

hologrambooks.com.au